CW00346167

Cara's happy-go-lucky life-style suited
her, and it was with amused pity that she
regarded the man in the smart suit who
left his office at the same time every
Friday and watched her busk in the
street. He, on the other hand, was stiffly
disapproving of her gypsy existence.
They were going in opposite directions –
yet somehow their lives began to
touch . . .

Another book you will enjoy
by ANN CHARLTON

THE DECEPTION TRAP

Since Ashe Warwick hadn't hesitated to walk
out on her when her family lost their money,
Teressa had had no conscience about deceiving
him when the occasion arose. Except that
the whole thing backfired on her rather
dramatically . . .

STREET
SONG

BY
ANN CHARLTON

MILLS & BOON LIMITED
15–16 BROOK'S MEWS
LONDON W1A 1DR

All the characters in this book have no existence outside the imagination of the Author, and have no relation whatsoever to anyone bearing the same name or names. They are not even distantly inspired by any individual known or unknown to the Author, and all the incidents are pure invention.

The text of this publication or any part thereof may not be reproduced or transmitted in any form or by any means, electronic or mechanical, including photocopying, recording, storage in an information retrieval system, or otherwise, without the written permission of the publisher.

This book is sold subject to the condition that it shall not, by way of trade or otherwise, be lent, resold, hired out or otherwise circulated without the prior consent of the publisher in any form of binding or cover other than that in which it is published and without a similar condition including this condition being imposed on the subsequent purchaser.

First published in Great Britain 1986 by Mills & Boon Limited

© Ann Charlton 1986

*Australian copyright 1986
Philippine copyright 1987
This edition 1987*

ISBN 0 263 75576 2

*Set in Times 10½ on 11 pt.
01-0287-49976*

Computer typeset by SB Datagraphics, Colchester, Essex

Printed and bound in Great Britain by Collins, Glasgow

CHAPTER ONE

THE very first time Cara saw him, he was on the escalator. Going up. There were any number of people on the escalator with him—any number on the downward bound one beside it on which she travelled. And all of them were doing what lift and escalator passengers did everywhere—avoiding eye contact with everyone else; staring at parcels, at backs, at heels on the steps above or below, depending on which direction they were taking. Eyes front, all of them. Except Cara and the man.

She noticed him as she stepped on at the top and he stepped on at the bottom. He consulted his watch, then looked up directly at Cara. There was a spark, a definite spark. She could only see his head and she supposed he could only see hers. Nice, she thought and her heart gave a bit of a bump. The moving stairs carried them towards each other and Cara had the weirdest feeling that the speed slowed down. His shoulders came into view: wide and chiselled in grey suiting. He wore a tie—not too loud, not too timid, just right. Suit jacket: creaseless. Shirt: pristine, pale blue, crisp. The vertical creases on his trousers were straight and sharp as a cutting edge. Shoes black and gleaming.

Her eyes came back to his as the stairs took them past each other. Their hands could have reached out and touched. Cara turned her head slightly. So did he. She smiled. He didn't. Then he was gone on his way up. She smiled wryly again, to herself this time; where

else would he be going? He looked the very epitome of
a man on his way up. A man of substance. Cara looked
down at herself. She wore flat sandals and a full, calf-
length skirt of Indian cotton, and a long, long
sleeveless top with a fringed sash wound around her
hips. Her hair was brown and sun-streaked and wind-
blown and curled half-way down her back, and the
only make-up she wore was a touch of gloss on her
mouth. Could there be two more complete opposites?
Cara alighted at the bottom and turned around. At the
top of the parallel escalator, the man looked over his
shoulder at her. He hitched a slim leather attaché case
under his arm and walked away. Cara tucked her flute
and a battered bowler hat under hers and did likewise.

'Danny Brand, ladies and gentlemen——' said Cara
later as Danny's last guitar note lingered. Flute under
her arm, she picked up the battered bowler and made
eye contact with a few late-night shoppers before they
could edge away. At her brilliant, encouraging smile,
two dropped money in the hat.

'One day you'll boast that you tossed a coin to
Danny,' she assured them. 'A legend in the making
right here in the heart of Brisbane—thank you, sir—
thank you, madam—come by next week, why don't
you? We're here every Friday night playing simply
magnificent music for you——' The crowd dispersed
along the city Mall and Cara turned to Danny, who
gave a modest smile. He wore tight jeans and a
flowered shirt and trainers without socks. A cowboy
hat was crammed down on his tufting blond hair.

'A legend in the making?' he queried drily. She put
down the bowler and flute and rummaged some
cartons of fruit juice from her bag which lay on the
marble steps of the Southdown Building behind them.

'Why not?' she laughed. 'You're much too reticent. Here, catch!' She tossed a carton to him.

' "Playing simply magnificent music"!' he said, pushing back his hat. 'You've got some cheek, Cara! I don't think I could bring myself to deliver a spiel like that.'

'You could if you didn't have me along—modest buskers make modest profits.' She bent to the pavement and gathered up the coins that had missed the hat or the guitar case. After a few quick calculations she said, 'It's going to be a "thirty" night at least—could go to forty. You'll be able to redeem Samantha soon.' Samantha was Danny's hot-shot, super deluxe Gibson electric guitar with the mother-of-pearl insets. He had pawned it when he'd lost his music shop job due to his boss becoming bankrupt and had fallen behind with his share of the rent. Although the flat they shared with Pete Gilbert was no palace, the rent was far from cheap, even split three ways. Danny needed his thirty- and forty-dollar busking nights. He got up and slipped an arm about Cara's waist.

'When I get Sam back I'll write "A Song for Cara". Without you I'd never be able to do this.' There was a serious note in his voice. All too often lately there was a serious note in Danny's voice. Cara shrank from it. Sharing a flat with two men was fine but it had to be on a 'just friends' basis.

'Sure you could. You have to be pushier—sell yourself to your audience. If you just sit there plucking away at your guitar like some moody, musical poet people will wander off without being given the opportunity to show their appreciation!'

He laughed. 'Beats me how you do it—one look from you, one smile and they put money in the hat!'

'So many people are shy,' she said gravely. 'They need a little encouragement.'

'You're so right.' He gave her a burst of melancholy from big blue eyes.

'Think of me as a sister, Danny boy,' she said lightly, 'An *older* sister.'

Danny groaned. 'So you've got two years on me—big deal! I'm twenty-three, all grown up. You might find you like younger men.'

'Ha! This is rebound stuff. When you get Samantha back you won't have any time for girls.'

'Always time for you, love.' He pulled her close and tried enthusiastically to kiss her on the neck. Cara laughed and jostled him away. She looked over his shoulder and that's when she saw the escalator man again. And he saw her.

He stood at the top of the Southdown Building steps just outside the bronze glass doors to the business suites that soared above the glitzy street-level boutiques and jewellers. There were three other men with him. The escalator man held Cara's gaze for a few moments. Even from here she saw the slight twist to his mouth as she shook Danny off and picked up her flute. They went into 'Duelling Banjos', a novel arrangement for guitar and flute, one that gathered a crowd very quickly. After a round of applause and a modest shower of coins Cara asked for requests in her usual breezy style, inverting her flute and moving around the crowd as if she was a reporter with a microphone.

'What about you, ma'am?' She stepped over to a buxom older woman hung about with shopping bags. 'Can we play a favourite song for you, Mrs——?' Mrs Franklin was her name, the woman volunteered, actually leaning slightly forward to speak into the flute.

'Um—well—the "Tennessee Waltz",' she said after some coaxing from Cara, 'but you're too young to know that one.'

'Too young? No such thing—we're really senior citizens, Mrs Franklin. Marvellous what a vegetarian diet can do.'

Danny disguised a cough of laughter and swept into the waltz-time rhythm. Cara sang, and when the lyrics momentarily eluded her she drafted in Mrs Franklin to help.

' "I remember the night and the Tennessee waltz——" ' they sang together, and Cara felt the man watching her. Her eyes wandered to him, wondering why she was interested. Normally she wouldn't look twice at someone like him. Cara didn't mingle with men who wore conservative grey and immaculate shirts—she didn't want to. He was one of millions who looked the same, yet there was something about him . . . attractive enough, she supposed. Not her type, of course; lord, no. Everything about him looked so strictly under control. As she watched, he shot back his cuff and consulted his watch. The other men fell about laughing at something. He smiled, but not enough to show any teeth. Maybe he didn't have time to laugh, she thought. Maybe he didn't have any teeth. But all jokes aside—there had been that spark for a few moments—something——

' "The bee-oo-ti-ful Tennessee waltz",' she finished in unison with Mrs Franklin of the shopping bags. The woman looked quite misty-eyed, and pressed a two-dollar note into the bowler, then went off looking twenty years younger. Cara got a kick out of that. Maybe she and Danny had revived a special memory for the woman, and maybe somewhere tonight in the suburbs a balding, overweight Mr Franklin would seem a little younger, a little more dashing.

'Requests—how about a top forty number?' asked Cara, doing her microphone bit again. She looked around for young Holly Kirby, but her problem pupil had gone. Most Friday nights she showed up with her school friends, partly for the novelty of seeing her music teacher performing and clowning around with bypassers, but also because she had a crush on Danny. Cara didn't expect that to last much longer. Holly was thirteen, and Cara remembered how fickle her own feelings had been at that age. Maybe her pupil's interest was already waning. Tonight she had disappeared without even a wave.

'You, sir——' Cara moved to a group of young men all sporting talkative tee-shirts, tutti-frutti-coloured pants and hairdos that defied Newton's laws of gravity and motion. 'Have you got a request?' she asked one. The boy guffawed, put his arm around Cara and made his request. A very explicit request. Oh dear, she thought—she really must think twice about giving openings to this age group. She resisted the urge to push the little monster away, smiling instead as Danny obligingly went into the nautical 'Portsmouth'. When she lifted her flute rather abruptly to play, her youthful admirer ducked, checked that his hair hadn't been damaged and gave up.

Coins rolled across the pavement and clinked in the bowler hat. As they finished the number, the crowd parted and a vigorous, husky figure in jeans and sleeveless vest burst through.

'She wrote!' he announced to the Mall at large and swooped on Cara, tossing her up into the air as if she were a seed dandelion.

'Put me down, Pete!' she shrieked as she went up for the second time. But Pete whirled her around, talking all the while, and she gathered that his girl-friend had written to him at last. The saga of Vivian and Pete had been going on for a while. Viv had tired of his reluctance for commitment and had gone off to do her own thing—back-packing around Britain. There had been a stony silence from her these last five weeks, during which time Pete had convinced himself that he would never get a second chance with Viv, and Cara and Danny had threatened to replace him with a less morose, self-pitying flatmate. Grinning from ear to ear, he set Cara down, catching her when she staggered dizzily.

'Great news, Pete,' she told him, patting his substantial tattooed arm. Pete was into body-building and it showed. His bare biceps bulged as he suddenly pulled her close and delivered a smacking kiss to her cheek.

'I wish she was here—I'd propose to her right now,' he beamed.

'You can always write a proposal,' suggested Danny. Pete's grin faded at once.

'Oh, I'm not very good at letters—I mean, I'd probably muck it up——'

'Coward,' Danny jeered, and broke into 'All My Friends Are Getting Married'. 'You'd better propose to her soon, mate. She might meet a passionate Pom over there——'

Pete just laughed.

'—or one of those big Swedes always hiking around Europe.'

'Nah.'

'A skier, I'll bet—one of those big, athletic guys in shorts——'

'It's autumn over there,' Pete reminded him.

Danny winked. 'Come on, mate, those Swedes don't feel the cold—inner fires—get my drift——?'

Cara tuned out of their badinage, and looked up. The escalator man was still there. He shook hands with the other men. His handshake was firm, duplicated exactly for each recipient and accompanied by one of those super-controlled half smiles. Another glance at his watch and he made his way down the steps. At the bowler hat he paused and felt in his pocket for change. Cara smiled encouragingly. 'I saw you on the Wintergarden escalator.'

'Oh yes?' he said as if he didn't remember.

'We were going in different directions.'

A slight twist of the lips at that. His eyes roamed over her clothes, her untamed mane of hair, the bowler hat.

'We would be, wouldn't we?' he said drily.

Cara laughed. 'Of course.' As he moved on she called, 'Did you enjoy our show?'

Cool green eyes flicked over her yet again—touched on Danny and Pete and shot back. 'I don't know,' he replied levelly. 'I'm still trying to decide what kind of show it is.' He tossed a gold coin in the bowler hat and walked away. Cara looked down at his money. It was the first time ever that she had felt diminished by someone's contribution.

The city's late trading closed at nine. Woolworth's mesh grilles clanked closed and doors disgorged last customers. The Mall was quieter when Danny, Cara and Pete walked through the potted palms and leopard trees. Lights glowed and the city slowed in the mild tropical spring night.

'Mmmm—smell that coffee . . .' They passed the crowded tables of Jimmie's on the Mall and crossed paths with Arty, the cockney fire-eater and juggler who worked a profitable Edward Street corner. Laden with his equipment, he called out without stopping, ' 'ow's business?'

'It'd be a lot better if you weren't pulling the crowds with that dragon act of yours, Arty,' answered Danny.

'All you need is a meths mouthwash and nerves of steel, old son,' said Arty. 'Oh—and it 'elps if you're crazy.' He laughed and went off, a circus figure in black singlet and baggy, braced trousers. The boys talked and Cara was silent.

Green eyes, she thought. A bit unexpected some-how in a face so disciplined. Rather frivolous of him to be green-eyed when clearly what was needed was grey to match that leanly fleshed bone structure, those dark, uncurving brows and that mouth. Bracketed by lines and set in slow-drying cement, that mouth was. Another couple of years and he might not be able to move it at all—

'—have you decided if you'll play?' Danny was asking her. She looked blankly at him. 'In that soirée old Strachan's planning for the Academy.'

'Oh, the soirée—yes, I'll be playing. I could hardly refuse, could I?' Mr Strachan, the principal of the Carrington Music Academy where she taught the flute, had a scheme to raise funds for scholarships for underprivileged, gifted children. Cara had agreed to perform, along with most of the other teachers, at a fund-raising soirée. 'Holly's father is hosting it, did I tell you that? You know Holly, your most devoted fan,' she teased Danny.

'Oh yeah, Holly. Now there's a rebel in the making.'

'Yes, well—her father's on the Academy's board, and he's offered his home for the occasion. He's in corporate law and loaded apparently, and he lives right in the heart of stockbroker country.'

'Loaded, huh? Not just middle-class comfortable?'

'Well—Holly *did* mention there was a peacock that ran around their lawns.'

'Oh, come *on*!'

When she parked her battered old khaki Mini outside their Red Hill flat, Cara reflected that they didn't even have a front lawn. Their Italian landlord had cemented it over to save all that time-consuming mowing. Ugly would be a kind word for the yard, and extravagant praise for the two-storey converted house.

'I really must speak to Mr Parini,' drawled Cara. 'A peacock on our concrete would make *all* the difference!'

Pete went to work on a canvas. Paint and turps and linseed oil were smells that Cara hardly noticed any more. He peered closely at his work in the single fluorescent light. No matter what they did, only one tube would light when switched on. The other smouldered for hours, would unexpectedly break into a wild disco flickering until with a demure 'brink' it would light up. It was in mid-smoulder at present.

Their flat was a cheerful jumble of three people's belongings and hobbies. Danny's acoustic guitars, banjo and bouzouki hung behind the divan with his cowboy hat. Pete was an art student and his painting corner looked like a bit of impressionist Montmartre; his finished canvases crowded over the awful walls. One of Cara's offbeat collages, strictly amateur and made for fun from throwaways, was also hung, and her poster of a Norfolk Island Boobook Owl, one of an endangered species series, faced the phone. The bird's huge, solemn eyes were a bit unsettling at times. Cara always had the feeling that the owl could see right through her.

She watered the pot plants that greened the flat. Whenever she moved on somewhere new she gave away her plants and collages and posters and started collecting and making all over again. Cara made a habit of travelling light. From Melbourne to Morocco, England, France, Greece—and back to Australia. France, she thought—Paris. Guy. She sighed, and went to water her window box of petunias.

'You'll have Miss Vernon complaining about them,' Pete said with a nod at the flowers.

'You think a dozen petunia plants could make a difference? She's been sneezing since July when the wattle came out and now her greatest dread of all: October is coming and the jacarandas are about to flower.'

'Thar she blows——' warned Danny, looking up from his guitar. Cara and Pete looked up too. From the flat above came a mighty 'ya-hoo!'.

When Miss Vernon first moved in they had pondered over this intermittent yell. Was it a cowboy from Texas re-living favourite rodeo rides? A football fan cheering his team's victory? But no one could have so many rodeo memories, and no one's football team so many victories. It was Miss Vernon's hay fever, and her sneezes were something of a miracle, coming as they did like a force ten gale from her scrawny, five-foot-one figure.

'It breaks me up the way you can tell in advance,' Pete commented to Danny.

'She runs for the tissue box—can't you hear her scampering from one side of the lounge to the other?' Danny raised a hand and tracked Miss Vernon's usual route with an index finger. 'And now an encore—wait for it——'

'Ya-hoo-oo!'

Danny hung up his guitar, took the bouzouki from the wall and began a Greek folk song. The tears-and-laughter music was irresistible. Cara put down her watering can, raised her arms and danced. After a while Pete dropped his brushes and linked arms with her, flourishing his paint-spattered rag. 'Onassis!' he shouted, and 'Melina Mercouri!'—his contribution to the Greekness of the occasion. Danny laughed and picked up tempo, playing faster and faster until they surrendered.

'You disappeared in a hurry on Friday night, Holly,' said Cara four days later.

Holly Kirby shuffled a bit on one of the Carrington Academy's uncomfortable chairs. 'Oh—well, I had to meet Dad. He goes off his brain if I'm not where I'm supposed to be at exactly the right time, know what I mean?' She grimaced. 'He wouldn't let me go into town at all except that I have basketball practice on Fridays and miss the last school bus home.'

'So you go into the city with your friends and, what—wait for him to finish work?'

'Mmm. Except when he's going out with *Cleo*, of course—then I have to take a taxi home from school.' She said the name 'Cleo' in the same tone that she reserved for 'maths' and 'flute practice'—both of which she hated. Or said she hated. It was hard to tell with Holly which were her genuine gripes and which merely fashionable. 'I'm only here because Dad insisted I learn to play the flute,' she had said pugnaciously at their first lesson two months ago. She wanted to play the guitar, she said, but Dad said no. As he was on the board of Carrington's, which didn't offer guitar lessons anyway, flute it had to be. The very minor efforts Holly had made at her lessons had only

come about in the last month since Cara had been
busking in the Mall. This Holly considered to be
trendy and very non-establishment, and Cara assumed a status much above that of a mere teacher as a
result.

'Okay, let's hear your homework piece,' said Cara,
and bravely sat through a rendition of Schumann's
Humming Song that made her wonder if Papa Kirby
realised he was sitting on a powder keg. Holly's
dissatisfaction was in her eyes, her rebellion in every
note. She was fed up with everything, or so she said:
the super-expensive school she attended, her teachers,
her hair, her freckles. But Cara didn't think she was
fed up with the father who seemed too busy or too
insensitive, or both, to work through her problems
with her. Cara got the feeling that the girl was seeking
attention from him. Of course it might be unfair to
assume her father was at fault. Holly was at an age of
exaggeration, and the man was a widower. Bringing
up a teenage girl alone would be no easy job.

Holly finished her performance, and Cara enjoyed
the silence for a few seconds before taking her through
it again. Then she set a new, lively exercise for
homework.

'Do you think I'd look good with short hair, Cara?'
Holly asked suddenly as she packed away her flute at
the lesson's end. 'Really short, I mean. I want it spiked
in the front, but Dad won't let me.'

A path of eggshells opened up in front of Cara. If
Holly was seeking an ally against her lone parent she
had to decline the position. 'Hmmm,' she studied
Holly's shoulder-length bob and stalled for time, 'let
me think——'

'Dad says it would look cheap.'

So it would, but good old Dad could use a little tact,

Cara thought. 'He probably loves your hair just the way it is, Holly.'

'He wouldn't notice if it was down to my ankles.'

'Oh, sure he would. You'd trip over it. *He'd* probably trip over it! And think of the shampoo bills. Even a man would have to notice.'

Holly giggled. '*Cleo* agrees with Dad, of course. She agrees with just about everything he says. She thinks if she does, he'll marry her. She's been waiting long enough.'

Maybe Daddy wanted a doormat, Cara thought. But it wasn't likely. This sounded like jealousy.

'What's she like?'

'Oh, you know—she's older, and blondeish, and she's a fashion buyer so she wears great gear, but, oh——' she wrinkled her nose, 'she's a bit of a drag, but the trouble is she doesn't really mean to be, and I always feel kind of guilty for thinking it. Don't you just hate people who make you feel guilty?'

'So she's nice?' Cara said, rather confused.

'*Awfully* nice. I wish she'd be rotten sometimes—I'd feel better about that, know what I mean?'

Cara said she thought she might.

'She was my mother's best friend. And she's my godmother,' added Holly unexpectedly. Cara wondered if the girl's mixed feelings about her godmother were due to the fear that she might become her stepmother. Picking up her schoolbag, Holly gave a sidelong grin and said goodbye.

'See you in the Mall on Friday then, Holly.'

The girl nodded and her shining, dark brown hair bounced.

'I'd think twice about spikes if I were you, but if you want a change why don't you talk to your father about it——'

'Ha! A lot of good *that* would do! He's just moved into a new office and hardly thinks about anything but work.'

'Maybe you're going about it the wrong way—he's probably tired when he comes home at night. Why not pour him a glass of wine and sit him down and talk to him, father to daughter——'

'Crawl, you mean?' Holly glared.

Cara was beginning to think that was what she would have to do to get a smile out of the escalator man. Her interest in him had crystallised into that one goal. The momentary spark between them had been a freak, killed off with the recognition that they were poles apart. But Cara was determined to see him smile. *Make* him smile. Each Friday night and, she supposed, every other night when she wasn't around to witness it, he followed the same routine. He appeared with one or more colleagues on the Southdown steps, checked his watch, talked a while, shook hands with firm precision, then looked up and down the Mall from his vantage point as if searching for someone. Then he came down the stairs and tossed a coin in the bowler hat. Cara was irked by it. She couldn't help feeling that the gesture was anything but appreciation for their music. More likely it was to rid himself of some nuisance small change or stemmed from some deep-rooted feeling of *noblesse oblige*.

She had tried her most dazzling smiles on him. Offered to play his favourite music.

'Can we play a request for you?' she had asked, stepping in front of him one night as he tossed money in the hat and walked on. He looked mildly surprised to find her barring his way, swiftly inspected her turquoise cotton sundress worn strapless and braless, and shook his head. The negative response was as much to the way she looked as to her question, she decided, grinning at him. Well, she certainly didn't expect Mr Conservative himself to approve of her taste in clothes.

'You do *have* a favourite song?' she prompted, trying to imagine him letting himself go to music. Did he ever sway a bit to pop or rock, dance to Latin—secretly conduct the Boston Philharmonic in his den? Yes, the last was more likely. 'A classical piece, perhaps?'

'No, thanks; I haven't the time,' he said, and as if to confirm it, a series of high-pitched electronic shrieks came from his wrist. He shot back his cuff and pressed a gold button to de-activate the watch alarm. Cara stared at the timepiece. Never had she seen so many digits, modal-variation buttons, grids and dials on a watch. It looked like a miniature dashboard of a Star Wars spacecraft. Did he program it—or did it program him?

'Hi—have you decided what kind of show it is yet?' she asked the next time she saw him, reminding him of that earlier comment. He blinked a bit at her cerise shirt and matching scarf wound Arab-style around her head. Cara winced at his immaculate superfine and crisp shirt, the immovable tie. Didn't the man ever look as if he lived in his clothes?

'I—think I've reached a conclusion,' he said in a slow, deep voice. Reached a conclusion, for heaven's sake, as if he was a jury member or a judge!

'And the verdict?' she enquired perkily, aware of Danny's frowning attention. He wasn't too pleased with her continuing interest in the escalator man.

'I'm broadminded,' the man told her, 'and your music's good. Let's leave it at that.'

Arrogant devil! She gave a servile little bob.

'Ever so glad our music pleases you, sir—can we play a request for you?'

'No,' he said, and made to move on. She darted in front of him, singing softly, 'Your lips tell me no, no— but there's yes, yes in your eyes——" ' Her laughter broke out. If there was yes, yes in *his* eyes, then there were little green men on the moon. His lips twitched. Cara waited with bated breath. He was *amused*. Any minute now he might actually smile. But it didn't get that far. There was a speculative light in his eyes though, as if he considered the option. Then he looked at Superwatch.

'How about "As Time Goes By"?' she suggested, feeling some deep, illogical aversion to his watch, 'or "The Sunshine Of Your Smile"?' He didn't take the hint but looked thoughtfully upwards.

'There is an old song I like—something about a lady——'

' "She's a Lady"?'

He shook his head.

' "Lady Love"?'

'No—"The Lady is——'

'A Tramp",' she supplied. He turned his head to look down at her.

'That's the one,' he said softly, and tossed a few coins in the hat. Then went.

It was one of those perfect nights that were repeated over and over in Queensland's spring. The air was soft and tender, warm promise of a blistering tropical summer to come, but kind as yet. The city was alive with people strolling, rushing, eating, meeting. Children laughing, crying. Parents watching, warning, drying. Endless variety. People fat and thin, scruffy and smart. A black-haired Asian family, freckled, tow-haired Australian kids. A dedicated drunk, his

identity blurred by the bottle. Trendies in tight little
groups, mods in modules of four or five, a mini city
tribe of Aborigine boys, huddles of high school kids in
checkered uniform, two baby-faced policemen with
two-way radios. Neon signs blinked, window displays
beckoned. In the windows of 'Mrs Brown's' in the
overhead walkway, Mall watchers drank *cappuccino*
coffee and ate raisin toast, and the electronic billboard
tack-tacked away on the Wintergarden complex,
weaving coloured messages and removing them with
computerised impartiality. Down past the Hilton at
the Edward Street end of the Mall, a great orange and
yellow gout of flame shot skywards. Arty was into his
act. Cara smiled and looked up. Stars glittered in the
strip of sky hemmed in by city towers. It was easy to
forget to look up at the stars in the neon blaze of a city,
but Cara never forgot. Not since Paris—because in
Paris there had been Guy. Nights like this always
reminded her of him. For the first time in two years
though, the poignancy of a warm spring night brought
memories and drifts of remembered music, but did not
sustain them. She couldn't get one song out of her head
no matter what else she played with Danny.

'She likes that free, fresh wind in her hair——' And
she couldn't rid herself of a tiny, astonishing hurt. The
escalator man was everything she both disliked and
pitied—arrogant, blinkered. Maybe rigid. A man who
knew where he was going but might have forgotten
why. To be misunderstood by a man like that was
inevitable, even desirable. '—she's broke—that's
oke——' The Lady is a Tramp! There was a chance
she could be misunderstanding him, of course. The
man might not have meant it as an insult. He might
genuinely like the song.

'—hates California, it's cold and it's damp——'

Ha! And there were little green men on the moon.
'—that's why the lady is a tramp.'

'Loaded' was certainly the right term for Holly's
father, Cara decided on the night of the soirée as Mr
Strachan's assembled small orchestra paused between
pieces. In an exclusive western suburb, Mr Mitchell
Kirby's house was set on a small acreage. Two-storied,
with colonnaded verandas upstairs and down, the
house was swathed in cerise and cream bougainvil-
laea. There was a Mediterranean flavour about the big
slate-floored patio lit by triple-globed lamps and
partly overhung by a grape-vine-twined pergola.
Spotlights shone on a Bechstein grand and on the
orchestra. From the patio's natural stage, the lawn
swept down to an underwater-lit pool, all rich and
milky aqua—and rose again in terraces conveniently
wide enough to take tables and chairs at which the
guests were eating their Sole Meunière and their
Meringues Chantilly.

A stir among the guests preceded the casual
entrance of the peacock. It minced by the pool, tail
swishing along the pale slate. As if conscious it had
centre stage, the bird suddenly elevated its tail, fanned
it out into a brocaded, sequinned beauty that made
every designer dress present drab by comparison. A
photographer took the remarkable picture: the bird
posing, its reflection shimmering in the pool with the
human socialites coming in a poor second behind it.

Cara sat with the other musicians. Tonight she was
nicely conformist in her pencil-slim black skirt and a
rather delicious flounced white blouse that she wore
for her occasional orchestra dates. Mr Strachan hadn't
been able to hide his relief when he saw her looking so
demurely conventional. He deplored her 'hippy'

clothes, as he called them, and often made terse suggestions about confining her hair. Usually she ignored them, but tonight she had made him very happy by pinning it up.

'You look *beautiful*, my dear,' Mr Strachan had gushed, overdoing it in his gratitude that she hadn't worn tie-dyed cotton and gladiator sandals. She didn't look beautiful—her mouth was too wide and her chin too square for beauty. But her thick brows, once the bane of her life, were now totally acceptable thanks to Brooke Shields and the like, and even her French music teacher—a miserable, sour man who'd hated the English and included Australians in his prejudice—had told her that her blue eyes were okay. '*Vous avez les yeux magnifiques*,' Monsieur Brabason had actually said in a moment of weakness. And he'd never seen her like this. Who knew what extravagant French compliment he might have offered her if she'd gone to his lessons with full make-up and her hair elegantly knotted.

She felt alien, and she disguised a grimace. Her toes wriggled around in the high-heeled shoes that she only ever wore to functions like this. Somehow she never really got used to them. Just as she conquered their treacherous wobbling on one outing, she took them off and put them away for another three or four months. Leaning down, she prised them off for a few moments of blissful freedom and looked out at the satinned, bejewelled, bow-tied guests. Her mouth fell open as one man caught her attention. A tall man with straight, dark hair. He was splendid in the black and white precision of a dinner suit, tucked shirt and bow tie that seemed somehow *neater* than all the other dinner suits, tucked shirts and bow ties. The escalator man? She shook her head, looked again. He walked towards the vine-hung patio and nodded to the musicians. His eyes panned across, paused on Cara for several seconds. A tiny frown—a 'Have I seen you before?' kind of frown, then he went to sit at a table with a striking ash-blonde woman.

He looked at his watch. Definitely the escalator man, Cara grinned. And she looked so respectable, so demure that he didn't even recognise her!

CHAPTER TWO

CARA played with the orchestra, took a break while a smaller ensemble dallied with Debussy. Every now and then the man glanced at her, a faint air of puzzlement about him. As soon as he saw her playing the flute, she had thought, he would make the connection. But no. Apparently he could not conceive that a wild-haired busker and this oh, so conventional classical performer could be in any way related. For her part she puzzled over the ash-blonde's place in the scheme of things. A wife, perhaps? But of all the rings adorning the lovely hands that touched his and held on to his arm, none were on her third finger, left hand.

Her solo came up and she took centre stage. Originally she had objected to performing the Chaminade *Concerto*, for personal reasons and because to her mind it was too blatant a showpiece for the flute. Now she looked forward to showing off a little.

Half-way through the piece, the memories came. She was in a tiny room in Paris with the sounds of another impassioned French argument rising from the flat below—and in self-defence she was playing this piece faster and faster and Guy was playing it too . . . she could almost hear the notes of his violin as he followed her brilliantly through the music he didn't know. Their performance had terminated that Gallic argument. The couple downstairs had stuck their heads from their window and applauded . . . Cara blinked. The applause was here and now. She had finished playing. But Guy had finished playing for

26

ever. Like warm spring nights, this music brought him
back, and like the music, the remembrance usually
lingered on. Tonight though, her memories retreated
as she looked to see the reaction of the escalator man.
He applauded in the same measured way he did
everything else. Cara smiled, wondering what he
might do if she passed around the bowler hat right
now.

In a refreshment break for the musicians, Holly
emerged just long enough to ask her to join her and a
few girl friends in the house when her performance
was at an end. She was gone before Cara could ask her
to point out Mitchell Kirby to her. She looked around
wondering which of these successful men might be the
corporate lawyer whose practice kept him in peacocks. He must be one of the people at Mr Strachan's
V.I.P. table. Mr Strachan liked to keep close to the
people who mattered. That distinguished man, thinning on top. Yes, that must be him. Of course it
explained Strachan's immense relief that she had
dressed for the occasion. If Mitchell Kirby wanted to
meet his daughter's teacher, Strachan would be
snobbishly mortified to introduce a 'hippy'. It said a
lot for her musical prowess that she'd been entrusted
with Kirby's daughter at all, Cara thought.

After she had played some arias from *The Magic
Flute*, Cara took her final bows. Her broad smile at the
escalator man brought a frown to his brow, but no
recognition. Really, Cara thought—it would be an
unkindness to leave him in ignorance. Retreating
beneath the grapevine, she lifted her flute and played
the first four bars of 'The Lady Is A Tramp'.

He jerked around as if he'd been shot. Cara laughed
and went to join Holly and her friends, who were
dancing to a Pointer Sisters' number in a ground floor

room of casual Berber-carpeted magnificence.

Large cushions had been dragged from the couches
on to the floor to encircle platters of potato crisps and
sausage rolls and some messy-looking tomato sauce.
There were a couple of ashtrays there too, with more
stubs in them than Cara would have expected to see at
an adult party.

Holly changed the tape when she came in. 'Hey, it's
an oldie,' she said cheekily. 'I'll put on some dance
music from your era, Cara——'

It was a Charleston. Holly giggled at Cara's
pretence at outrage. 'Can you dance to that?' she
asked.

'Can't everyone?' Cara sucked in her cheeks,
pursed up her lips to a pouty twenties bow and
shimmied into her repertoire of Charleston steps. She
hitched up her skirt for some side kicks, she side-
hipped, thigh-slapped and black-bottomed.

'Ooh-boop-a——' Cara cried in a squeaky flapper
voice and spun around, vamping. She stopped in mid-
shimmy.

'—doop,' she finished face to face with the escalator
man. He was astonished, staring at her flushed face,
the strands of curling hair stuck to her damp temples
and neck. She blinked a bit. His astonishment turned
to annoyance. It occurred to her that he must be a
friend of the Kirby family to simply follow her into the
house uninvited like this. Holly fidgeted, then stepped
forward.

'Dad,' she said, 'this is my music teacher, Cara—I
mean Miss Matheson.'

The Charleston rhythm romped on, mad and
frivolous and hysterically inappropriate for this
revelation. Dad-dad, Dad-dad, Dad-dad, da-da Dad-
dad—Holly switched off the tape and Cara and

Mitchell Kirby stared at each other.

'Music teacher?'

'Dad?' she panted. Him? Mitchell Kirby should have thinning hair and look more—more *fatherly*. Fathers of teenage girls had no right to look so intriguing. She looked from him to Holly to see the similarities she'd not noticed before. The green eyes, the straight, dark brown hair—a certain something about the chin. She eyed him cautiously. Right now he looked as if he'd taken a punch on that chiselled chin. Her sense of humour bubbled. First he'd seen her as a busker, then as a perfectly proper performer on his patio, and now he was faced with this third dimension as his daughter's music teacher. And she had to be boop-a-dooping a Charleston! No wonder he looked a bit glassy-eyed. Laughing, she held out her hand.

'So we're introduced at last. Now I can stop calling you the escalator man.'

'The what?' Plainly disconcerted, he took her hand in an automatic male reflex. Cara studied him. She liked him disconcerted; he forgot to look so snooty. 'I had to think of you by some name for Friday nights,' she explained.

Holly bit her lip, darted an odd look at Cara. Ah—it began to make sense. Daddy might be broadminded, but he'd probably told his daughter not to hang around the buskers. Which could explain why, when he appeared on the scene, she disappeared. And why Holly hadn't revealed that her music teacher played on the street.

'I might not have recognised you,' Mitchell Kirby said, eyes narrowed, 'but for those last few bars of music you played.'

Cara grinned. 'My signature tune? If I'd known who you were I might have decided to stay incognito.'

But she wouldn't. It would have been irresistible in any case.

From the corner of her eye, Cara saw one of the ashtrays do a slow slide along the carpet. Holly was nudging it out of sight, but she was too late. Her father saw the stubs and frowned.

'There'll be no more smoking here, girls,' he said abruptly. There was a sigh of resignation from one of the girls, a precocious little thing dressed to look sixteen rather than thirteen.

'Is that understood, Holly?' he added.

She shrugged, then nodded, giving her answer as reluctantly as possible to save face. Her friends looked expectantly at her as if they felt she might offer an argument. The precocious one looked contemptuous and the others embarrassed when she didn't, and Holly turned a deep red. Cara felt for her. Mitchell Kirby could have handled that better.

'I think we need to talk, Miss Matheson,' he said, turning back to her. She waved a hand at the girls and went out with him. He stopped at a bar in a breathtaking room full of paintings and beautiful furniture, asked her choice of drink, poured two and guided her outside. Instead of heading back to the peacock's terraces he led her via a side exit on to a path that meandered through a veritable jungle. Gold and green striped stems of bamboo creaked gently one upon the other and their brushstroke leaves rustled. There were lights at intervals along the stone walkway, glowing on shaggy trunks of tree ferns, giant lime and yellow leaves of devil's ivy, the deep copper underleaves of miniature date palms. Somewhere a bird called—a long, silver note ending in a chuckle. The music of the string quartet drifted through the tropical garden in mannered incongruity.

'Drums,' she said, glancing at him. 'There really ought to be the sound of jungle drums in here.' He gave her no answering smile, and Cara's nerves jumped. It occurred to her that Mr Mitchell Kirby might be reluctant to let her continue teaching his daughter. She felt quite alarmed at the idea of losing touch with Holly. There was some slender bond between them— something vague yet important. 'Where are we going?' she joked. 'Darkest Africa?'

No answer.

'If you wanted to talk, we could have done that inside.'

'I wanted to talk privately,' he said.

'Well—this is private.' She waved a hand around. 'Just you, me and the headhunters.'

No answer. She'd thought it quite amusing. The path merged into a large, flagged area which was forecourt to a crescent-shaped aviary that looked as if it had grown there among the bamboo and banana trees, the piccabeen palms and thick, fragrant clumps of lemon grass. A large fig tree grew up through the cage, its lower branches leafed with magnificent birds. Even in the partial glow of garden lamps, Cara could see the brilliant plumage, elegant sweeps of tail feathers, the pale outline of a feather coronet cresting a head turned in profile. There was a rush of wings—a sound of rustling silk and flash of iridescent blue-purple followed by a raucous cry. A pure white cockatoo climbed up the mesh and tipped its head to watch them.

'Oh!' Cara breathed. She went closer, admiring then pitying the creatures as she always did anything caged. 'How beautiful. But how awful.'

'Awful?' he queried.

'Keeping them locked up.'

'You'd rather they were set free to die of hunger or be preyed on by cats? They'd die in days. They're not creatures of the wild.'

'Ah, but they should be,' she said sadly, leaning on the mesh. The cockatoo sidled along until it was level with her, then nibbled gently on her finger. When Cara looked up, Mitchell Kirby was watching her, a peculiar expression on his face. With a small sound of irritation he took a few paces away.

'What's your partner's name?' he asked. 'The cowboy guitarist.'

'Danny Brand.'

'And the other man—where does he fit in? The muscle-man with the tattoo?'

She smiled. 'Yes, it's a bit much, isn't it? A youthful mistake—the tattoo, I mean. His name is Peter Gilbert. He's a part-time art student. I live with him and Danny.'

She'd phrased it badly, she could see that. Mr Conservative construed 'living together' as something quite different.

'The three of you?' he said, with a twist to his mouth.

Oh, lord—*a ménage à trois*? Is that what he thought? Considering there had been no man in her life but Guy, not seriously anyway, that was almost laughable. But darn it, she wasn't going to explain. Her private life was no business of his.

'Uh-huh. The three of us. We share a flat in Red Hill.'

He walked away to sit on the garden seat positioned under a lamp. The light flowed over him from above, throwing his eyes into deepest shadow beneath the uncompromising brows, highlighting his bossy nose and the firm shape of his lower lip. Attractive enough, had she thought? He was sensational!

'Does your—art student friend have a job?' he
asked.

Cara noted the unflattering hesitation and bit back
a retort. The man couldn't help his attitude, she
supposed, and he *was* Holly's father. So she told him
about Pete's struggle to pay student fees, his stint as a
tutor himself, his occasional casual labouring work
and his two-nights-per-week-job at a sculpting class.

'What does he do there?'

'He's a life model.'

'A life model. Of course,' he said drily, as if posing
nude automatically meant taking part in some artistic
orgy. 'What about Brand—what does he do when he
isn't busking?'

'He's out of work right now—he writes music and
we're busking to try to raise the money to get
Samantha out of hock——' Cara smiled at his
bafflement. 'Samantha is his electric guitar.'

'Ah. So he writes rock music, I take it?' he said as if
it was pretty low stuff. 'And you're the only one with a
regular job.'

He wanted to know more—what she had done
before she took the teaching job at Carrington's. Cara
considered telling him it was none of his business, but
only briefly. She didn't mind talking here in the quiet
jungle garden. Not at all. He didn't seem impressed
with her lighthearted resumé of her various occupa-
tions in various locations. Waitress, typist, crop-
picker, tour guide, cook. She shrugged. 'If I can't find
a teaching job I take whatever work is available—
within reason.'

Mitchell Kirby watched her keenly, lifting his glass
to his lips now and then. He sat, one long leg thrown
across the other, one arm extended along the bench

back. A pose that betrayed a certain tension, Cara thought.

'And you *like* this life—roaming around, never settling anywhere?'

She grinned. 'Love it. You don't know what you're missing.'

'I'll take your word for it,' he said drily. 'Where were you a tour guide?'

'In Greece. Only for a couple of months. I took two groups of English and Australian tourists on a ramble through the ruins and villages—rucksacks and camping. A bit of a jaunt really. I only got the job because I spoke English and could manage some basic Greek and read road signs.' She laughed and went to sit down on the bench, swivelling to face him. 'But they vastly overrated *that* ability!'

'You got lost?'

'And how! We toiled fifteen kilometres in blinding heat one day before I discovered we'd gone the wrong way.'

'What did you do?'

'Oh—we came across a little village with a friendly taverna proprietor who had a cousin in Melbourne. And would you believe it—I'd actually been to his cousin's restaurant? Incredible, isn't it? Needless to say, Andreas treated me as if I'd stepped down from Mount Olympus. He was mine host with a vengeance when he found I had to save face—the Greeks understand about things like that. He showed us some ruins tucked away on a nearby hillside—just a couple of columns really, but with a legend attached. A bumbling tour guide's dream.'

'So your tourists forgave you?'

'Nope.' She laughed. 'I didn't tell them we were lost. They were having such a good time learning the local dances from Andreas' family and taking photographs of the ruins that I just let them assume I'd taken them there on purpose. It worked out so well that I *did* take the next tour there on purpose. Andreas was delighted. Sold three months' supply of ouzo in a couple of weeks.'

'You've got a nerve,' he said, shaking his head. 'Were you in Greece before or after you lived in Paris?'

'It was after . . . how did you know I lived in Paris?'

'Strachan told me. Naturally before I sent Holly for lessons I checked out the flute teacher.' He paused. 'He didn't mention you were a busker, too.'

'He wouldn't. Mr Strachan's a snob. He feels good music is for the worthy, not to be just given away or paid for in pennies.'

Mitchell Kirby eyed her thoughtfully as if he might comment, but didn't allow himself the distraction.

'He said you'd won a very prized scholarship to study in Paris. You must have been outstanding. I can't understand why you simply drift around——'

'You can learn a lot by just "drifting around",' said Cara. 'In Paris I worked hard enough trying to please my miserable teacher, but it was the drifting around that taught me what really mattered. Bus trips into the country, watching the sword-swallowers at the Centre Pompidou, rambling through the parks and the Louvre and sunbaking by the Seine. And busking, of course, in the Metro tunnels——'

Busking with Guy. Parisians rushing in timetable tides to the trains . . . his violin notes a-dance over the clickety-click of the ticket machines and the thunder of the underground. Guy, his bony face tilted over his violin, eyes alight with mischief as he quickened the tempo of a romantic piece to a dash and a gallop to match the pace of the last-minute boarders. And herself, lowering her flute, most times from laughter, holding out the battered bowler for a few hastily flung francs . . .

'Life really is a game to you, isn't it?' Mitchell Kirby said. 'I presume there was a man to ramble through the parks with.'

Cara took a sip of her drink, stalling. 'Of *course* there was a man,' she said, faintly shocked. 'We're talking about Paris—city of lovers!'

'Someone special?'

'Yes, Guy was someone special.'

'So you had, what—six months, a year with him. What then?'

What then? He'd died, that's what then. A young man with the gift of music and the gift of living. It didn't hurt so much any more, but the memory was too tender to touch upon with this cool, ungiving man.

'Then—it was over.'

'Your Paris affair?' he asked drily.

You poor man, she thought. You just don't have a clue. Flippantly she said, 'Right. Like you said—life's a game.'

Silence fell. His glass was cradled in his palm, the stem threaded through his fingers. He looked along the bench at her and in the jungly half light of the garden their eyes held. Reality slipped away from her for a few seconds . . . he was not Mitchell Kirby, Holly's father, corporate lawyer—just a man who made her nerves leap to attention. That spark—the spark that had leapt between them that very first time on the escalator—was there again. Cara stood up hastily.

A few drops of her drink spilled, and she set down her glass on the seat and brushed off her skirt, concentrating on the task. Her hand shook a bit. A spark between her and Mitchell Kirby? Crazy. Since Guy had died, she'd wondered if she would ever experience again that immediate flare of attraction to a man. This must be a freak. Some weird electrical current gone haywire. She could never be drawn to someone like this. Her heartbeat raced as she heard Mitchell Kirby stand up and walk over to her.

'You seem shy suddenly,' he said with a sardonic note in his voice. 'Not afraid I might take up all your unspoken invitations, are you, Miss Matheson?'

Her head shot up. 'Invitations?'

'You've been very persistent——' he murmured, head to one side. 'If you didn't play your games with so many, I might even be flattered.'

Cara's mouth dropped open. She set her hands on her hips. 'You don't think I've been making a *play* for you, surely?'

'Miss Matheson, I'm a modest man, but I know when I'm being pursued.'

Her sound of astonishment disturbed the birds. 'Fancy yourself as irresistible, do you, *modest* Mr Kirby? Let me tell you that if I chased a man with some—some relationship in mind, it wouldn't be a stuffed shirt like *you*.' Her index finger jabbed at his chest for emphasis. 'Shall I tell you why I tried so hard with you? It was because I wanted to see if you could actually *smile*'.

He gave a snort of disbelief that sent her temper sky high. She wasn't entirely sure why the whole business angered her so—Mitchell Kirby seemed to have struck a nerve.

'Yes, *smile*! You look as if you've forgotten, or never learned how—I can't decide which. *You*, Mr Kirby——' she gave another jab to his chest, which appeared to annoy him, '—look as if you've come off an assembly line somewhere.' Disparagingly she waved a hand at his evening clothes. 'Swish, zip, zap! Not a crease, not a speck—clothes just right. The conservative *Vogue* man. Programmed for success— smiles an optional extra!' She craned her neck, stuck her face pugnaciously close to his. 'I wasn't *flirting* with you, escalator man, I was trying to coax a bit of life into you, because, you know what? I feel *sorry* for you!'

It floored him. 'Sorry for me?' he echoed, on a rising note. 'You—sorry for *me*?' He caught at her arms as she made to move away. 'How dare you feel sorry for me?'

His arrogance, his outrage at the very idea, almost made her laugh, but his grip on her arms firmed, lifting her up on to her toes, and she had to force the humour.

'Ridiculous, isn't it? The likes of me, pitying the likes of you. Sorry! Oops, there I go again, just can't seem to stop using that word——'

He clicked his tongue in exasperation and gave her a tiny shake. Her uncertain heels wobbled. One turned over. With a little yelp she clutched at him for support, standing on one leg while she swung the other back to inspect her shoe. 'Oh, darn it,' she muttered, 'the tip's come off—look——'

Mitchell Kirby peered over her shoulder at the high heel, then abruptly drew back, patently annoyed that he had obeyed the compulsion to look.

'Fascinating, I'm sure, but I have guests and——'

'Oh. Oh——' Cara exclaimed as his sharp withdrawal shook her stork-like position. Her raised foot came down in a hurry, the untipped heel lodging unerringly in a join in the flagging. She stood for a

moment, trying to drag the shoe free, arms wavering
as if she was a tightrope walker trying to strike a
balance, then she reached out for the nearest solid
object. Mitchell Kirby. Or rather, Mitchell Kirby's
lapels.

'For God's sake—don't try to wrench it free—take
your foot out of the shoe and you can——' But it was
too late to do anything so sensible. Cara was falling—
falling—backwards, and though she scrabbled at his
lapels and he grabbed at her waist, she kept right on
falling in slow motion, wincing in anticipation of the
impact. But she missed the flagstones and landed in a
patch of garden that was mercifully cushioned by a
ground cover of ivy. It even bounced a bit beneath her.
The impact came when Mitchell Kirby sprawled to
the ground. Right on top of her.

'Uhh!' All her breath left her; she was pressed down
into the ivy and felt the network of stringy stems bite
into her back. Mitchell Kirby's head came to rest on
her chest. Her arms closed involuntarily around his
shoulders.

Drums, she thought, dragging in a breath. Way off
somewhere in another world, musicians were playing
Beethoven's Violin Concerto. Here there were drums.
A tattoo of them, low and mellow. Bamboo leaves
rustled, the stems creaked and sang as the breeze
shifted them, lifted them this way and that. A bird
fluttered softly in the cage. The air was evening cool
now. Cara was warm. Hot.

Her flounced blouse had slipped a button, pulled
askew to expose half her chest and a shoulder.
Mitchell Kirby lifted his head and his lips skimmed
across the bare skin between her breasts, his breath
huffed warm all the way up to her shoulder. His eyes

roamed over the path he'd taken, dragged at last up to her face.

'Are you hurt?' he asked huskily.

Her ribs were bruised, his shoe had caught her ankle a painful blow, but she shook her head, staring at him as he stared at her. He made no further attempt to move. His body lay over hers; his heart slammed away against her. Her legs were every which way, tangled with one of his between. A man in a dinner suit and bow tie, she thought, the escalator man himself, was lying here in the undergrowth with her in an attitude of abandonment. It should be funny. She sought a neat phrase, a joke to put the whole thing in perspective, but he reached up and lifted a heavy strand of hair from her forehead, and Cara's hands slid languidly across his shoulders and his eyes went to her mouth and hers to his. He couldn't kiss her, she thought dizzily—his mouth was set in slow-drying concrete . . . but it certainly looked softer now . . . parted and almost sensual, close and closer and God, he *was* going to kiss her and it was going to be good, she just knew it, and already she wanted to kiss him back——

Beep! Beep! Beep! Mitchell Kirby's head jerked up. With an exclamation he pushed back his cuff and pressed a button on Superwatch. The alarm stopped. Cara began to laugh. A spark, she'd thought. A spark! Between her and this computerised, regulated man of business! Thank God for Superwatch. It had restored her to sanity. Her laughter brought a thunderous frown to Mitchell Kirby's face. Muttering under his breath, he twitched her blouse over her shoulder as if the sight of her disarray offended him. Impersonally he fastened the undone button, then stood and pulled her up. They spent a few seconds brushing themselves off, and she heard him mutter something again. His lapels might never be the same again. Cara's amusement broke through now and then in small muffled coughs. Mitchell Kirby removed her shoe from the flagging, and held it out to her.

'I feel a bit like a down-market Cinderella,' she laughed. 'A damaged shoe instead of a glass slipper— electronic beeps from a wristwatch instead of majestic chimes of a clock at midnight——'

'Me instead of Prince Charming.'

'Good lord—is that humour I hear?' she exclaimed in mock surprise. He favoured her with a long, steady look, then consulted the watch, which had lapsed into passivity. Cara wondered if his frequent checks were to calculate how much time he'd spent—or how much he had left.

'I must rejoin my guests. I'd prefer you didn't see Holly again tonight.' Snip, snip the words went. He turned to walk away and Cara caught his arm.

'Just a minute——'

'What is it?' he asked sharply as she came close. Anyone would think he was afraid of her. Cara picked an ivy leaf from his hair and showed it to him.

'What *would* your guests have thought?' she mocked.

With an exclamation he strode off along the path.

'I won't tell if you won't,' she called after him, but there was just the click of his heels and the swish of the bamboo at his passing. On the empty garden seat their two almost empty glasses sat. At opposite ends.

Holly Kirby was not at her next music lesson on Tuesday. On Wednesday Cara discovered that Holly had been removed from her student list and was now assigned to the other flute teacher. She was hurt, annoyed, but not entirely surprised. Mitchell Kirby had made it clear that he didn't approve of her life-style even if—as he claimed—he was broadminded. Apparently his broadmindedness did not extend to letting his daughter mix with her. Cara's mood progressed from hurt to indignation to regret that she would have no further contact with Holly.

On Thursday, pay-day, her mood passed abruptly from regret to rip-roaring wrath. Because on Thursday Mr Strachan fired her. It was fantastic, incredible! To have Holly removed from her tutelage—all right. But to have her, Cara, removed from the Academy was an arrogant, rotten thing to do. She thought of her modest savings and the rent to pay and the new silencer she needed for the Mini, and she thought of the chances of picking up another teaching job now with less than two months until the school summer holidays, and her anger shot up, burst like fireworks inside her head.

'I take it Mr Kirby has been talking to you,' she snapped.

'I can't ignore a complaint from one of our directors, Miss Matheson,' said the little man, fussing around with his silver pens and pencils. 'Especially one as active and supportive as Mr Kirby.'

Of course he couldn't. Mr Kirby had offered a no-strings scholarship in addition to hosting the soirée. Mr Kirby had money and influence—and Mr Kirby had spoken! Cara collected her things and left. She decided to take her complaints to the source. Right away while her anger still boiled.

CHAPTER THREE

KIRBY, GRANTHAM & KIRBY had offices on the twelfth floor of the Southdown Building on the Mall. A signwriter was at work on the glass doors, filling in the outlines of the new tenant's name with gold-leaf. Inside, the signs of Mitchell Kirby's recent move here were few. Already the office looked prosperous, permanent. Fleecy carpet, glossy chrome, lush ribbed upholstery, several late-model typists operating late-model processors and an elegant, earlier-model receptionist politely barring access.

'Mr Mitchell Kirby,' Cara said firmly. 'Its personal.'

The woman was not moved. In one quick glance she had totted up the value of Cara's clothes and found the total less than the magic fee of entry; she might never have got past that lady had not a door opened to reveal Mitchell Kirby sitting at a desk. A young man emerged, stepping back as Cara, spotting her target, shot past him. Mitchell Kirby looked up sharply, frowned at Cara, then nodded to the young man who lingered like a watchdog.

'It's all right. Close the door, Craig.' He leaned back in his magnificent chair, surveyed her jeans and baggy peasant blouse and her hair which clouded around her face and over her shoulders. She flicked it aside and it crackled.

'What can I do for you, Miss Matheson? I suppose I can safely take it this isn't a professional consultation.'

She took a deep breath. 'You can't think of a single

43

reason why I should be here, Mr Kirby?' she said with
deceptive mildness. God, how she hated him. He was
so—neat. So—groomed! Not a hair of that glossy dark
head out of place. Not a crease on his shirt. His tie was
knotted perfectly and sat smugly straight. No jacket
today, the first time she had witnessed the pheno-
menon. But, jacket or not, he was the epitome of good
male grooming. For some reason it fanned her fury.
She would love to see some sign that he suffered from
the problems of normal people—a splash of coffee on
that pale blue shirt, a smudge of ink on his fingers, a
ruffle of hair over one ear.

He sighed. 'If I tried I might come up with
something, I suppose, but I'm a busy man, Miss
Matheson, and I don't have time for guessing games.
Why don't you tell me?' He consulted Superwatch and
she gritted her teeth.

'Going to set the alarm? How much time will you
allot to me—do I get five minutes before the beeps
go?' She leaned her hands on his desk and glared at
him. Mitchell Kirby regarded her as if she was a bit
loony or delirious, and got up as a telex machine
behind him began to clack.

'You seem a bit distraught—perhaps if you get it all
off your chest quickly, hmmm?' he suggested, and
turned his back to her to read the incoming message. 'I
find it hard to believe all that pent-up emotion is
because you won't be teaching Holly any more.'

'And why *won't* I be teaching her, Mr Kirby?' she
gritted. Was he going to deny responsibility—blame it
on Mr Strachan?

'It was a matter of practicality. Tuesday lessons no
longer suit Holly because of—extra school studies.
You were fully booked with students on other days, so
she had to change teachers.'

'Bull!' she snapped. The hypocrite—he was going to pretend he knew nothing about her being fired. He swung around from the telex with a torn off message in his hand. 'You don't think I'm a fit person for your daughter to associate with because you don't like the way I live——'

Mitchell Kirby pressed his intercom button. 'Come in, would you, Valerie?' he said while Cara took a frustrated turn around his office. 'We've got a problem with the Barrett copyright case.'

'—because I share a flat with two men—*platonically*, I might add, though it's none of your damned business—and just because Danny and I sing in the street so we can buy back Samantha——'

Valerie came in on this, wide eyes flicking from Cara to her boss, curiosity disguised beneath the pleasant impassiveness of the perfect secretary. Mitchell Kirby briefly outlined some action to be taken as a result of the telex.

'—and just because Pete models nude for a sculpture class——' Cara went on as soon as their business was finished. Valerie gave a startled little double-take before she closed the door.

'—you seem to think I'm some kind of—of—moral degenerate! Well, you're *wrong*!' She crashed her fist down on his desk just as Valerie put her head in the door again. The woman winced and asked a question, to which Mitchell merely nodded. The door closed. There was a marked silence from the word processors outside.

He studied Cara, appeared to reach some decision. 'All right, I'll level with you,' he said. 'The fact is, I don't like your life-style, but it doesn't bother me. Why should it? You appear to be happy drifting around, wasting your life and your talents——' He held up his hands as she opened her mouth to protest. 'Let me finish, Miss Matheson,' he said softly in the manner of a teacher talking to an over-excited child. 'What you choose to do has no effect on me. I'm an adult with fully formed views and values; your approach to life appears to me for what it is. A juvenile opting out of responsibility, a refusal to become involved permanently with anyone or any place out of—oh, laziness, cowardice—I don't know what your specific problems are.'

Cara cast her eyes upwards. 'Oooh!' she cried deep in her throat. 'Of all the prigs—you smug, arrogant devil! You spend *your* life at the beck and call of machines and—and a *watch*!' She jabbed a hand at these items, at his phone that had begun to ring. 'And you think you're really living, don't you, you stuffed shirt!'

'Be that as it may——' he said, infuriatingly calm, 'our problem here is *your* way of life, not mine—hello,' he said into the phone. Agitated, she strode around his office while he talked, stopping to glance over his framed degree—Mitchell Robert James Kirby, it said, had satisfied the examiners. He would have three names, she thought. Very aristocratic of him. There were photographic portraits of two men—Robert James Mitchell Kirby and James Mitchell Robert Kirby. His father and grandfather, apparently. A good thing Mitchell Kirby had a daughter and not a son. They'd used up all the name combinations. Just what would he call a son if he ever had one? Something suitably stuffy. What else from a man who could say 'be that as it may'?

'Hold my calls, Valerie,' he said into the intercom when he'd hung up. 'Where were we?'

'We were up to my laziness and cowardice and your

stuffed-shirtedness,' she grimaced, and corrected herself. 'Your priggishness.'

'Ah, yes. The thing is, Miss Matheson, my daughter is *not* an adult with fully formed views and values. She is not yet fourteen, and is going through a difficult stage. She's told me now that she likes you, confides in you——'

'Shocking! We can't let her have someone she likes and confides in, now can we?' she sneered. 'What kind of a father would allow such a thing?'

His jaw clenched. Cara was glad to see he wasn't as calm as he appeared. 'Holly is kicking at the traces. To her your way of life might seem desirable—unconventional, anti-authoritarian, even glamorous. She has already run away from home once with some misguided notion that there was a better life elsewhere, and I can't risk having her influenced by someone like you.'

Cara's anger took a dive. 'Ran away? Holly? Oh heavens, no—when was that?'

He was taken aback by her swift switch to concern. 'Six months ago. She took money from my safe and went off with a girl friend to take a plane to Sydney——'

'Sydney!' Cara closed her eyes. 'Oh, lord! Two young girls adrift in Sydney—anything could have happened.'

He ran a hand over his hair and for a few moments he looked almost *distrait* at the memory. 'Believe me, I've had nightmares over it. Fortunately the airport counter staff alerted the police and the girls were— detained.' He shook his head as if to rid himself of the unpleasant business. 'Holly has promised me not to run away again, but her behaviour hasn't improved. She finds it hard to accept discipline and has abandoned her ambition to study law, I don't know why——' he shook his head again, at a loss. Then he looked at Cara. 'I can't have her using you as a role model. You have a lot of charm——' he hesitated, 'and your appeal makes you quite—dangerous.'

There was an odd little silence, during which their eyes held. Mitchell Kirby broke away first and checked the time, and her blood pressure started to soar again.

'I hope I've explained the matter satisfactorily to you, Miss Matheson, and I hope, if you should see Holly when you're performing in the street, that you won't encourage her——'

'You—insufferable prig!' Cara exploded. 'Someone *should* encourage her! It seems to me that your daughter could use some encouragement, a bit more warmth in her life. No wonder the poor kid ran away——'

'That's enough!'

'—she always seems to have plenty of money—is that responsible parenting? Giving her money instead of time?'

'I will not discuss my daughter——'

'And you really played the heavy about smoking, didn't you? The way you go about it is just likely to make her *want* to smoke just to save face with her friends!'

'That's *enough*!'

Cara thrust her face up to his. 'She told me she can't even talk to you about things that worry her——'

'How dare you——'

'—you'd do better to look to your own influence instead of worrying about mine, and——'

'*Shut—up*!' he roared, grabbing her by the shoulders and shaking her. 'I will not listen to advice about my daughter from a cheap little itinerant——'

Cara heaved herself from his grasp. She threw her right hand at him and didn't bother to open it. Her fist glanced off his jaw, taking him by surprise. Flinching, he staggered off balance, a hand to his face. Astonishment turned to fury and she took one step backwards, then another as he came for her. Cara's heart thudded. Suddenly he looked a lot bigger. How come she hadn't noticed that his impeccable shirt collars circled a broad, strong neck? Those shoulders looked muscly without his perfect tailoring and he had long arms. Too long. He grabbed and caught her and she gabbled, 'You deserved it ... don't you touch me——'

He hauled her in, fingers biting into the flesh of her upper arms, his hold dragging on the fabric of her blouse. Cara felt the wide, elasticated neckline pull out over one shoulder. Her head snapped back, then fell forward, and her face pressed for a moment against his neck and a subtle spicy smell of aftershave filled her nostrils. Her heart was hammering away like a metronome at prestissimo. 'I'm warning you,' she said, raising her head to glare at him, 'you can't manhandle me and—and——'

Mitchell Kirby's angry eyes slid sideways to her bared shoulder and Cara faltered. '—and get away with it,' she finished breathlessly as he appeared to become absorbed with the view of bare skin. On her arms the tips of his fingers moved in sequence as if he was playing a five-finger piano exercise. Slowly his gaze roved right across the wide, stretched neck of her blouse, then up to her face. There wasn't a sound. No keyboards humming in the outer office, no phones, no voices. Just the deep silence of speculation. Even the telex was silent. Mitchell Kirby lifted her on to her

toes; her hands slid upwards from his chest to the
juncture of his neck and shoulders. His breath mingled
with hers. The warmth of his mouth was just—a—
whisper—away.

The world got moving again. The telex burst into
electronic chatter. His intercom buzzed once. Twice.
Outside, two phones began to ring in tandem. Mitchell
Kirby dropped her as if she was a hot coal. He strode
around behind his desk, adjusting his tie, adjusting his
face. Valerie said a few words over the intercom.

'Thanks, Val—no, I have the number.' He consulted his watch, pressed a mode button and jotted down
some figures from the dial. God, it even listed phone
numbers for him, Cara thought, shakily re-arranging
her blouse. 'Come in anyway, will you, Valerie?' he
added as he picked up one of his phones. With some
satisfaction, Cara observed that he wasn't the same
man who had so annoyed her when she'd come in.
There was a crease on his shirt now, all right. His hair
had flopped a fraction and on his jaw was the red mark
of her fist. Best of all, there was a smudge of her
lipstick on his collar. The man looked almost human.
He began to jab out numbers on the phone. 'See Miss
Matheson out, will you, Val?' he said without looking
up when his secretary rather cautiously opened the
door.

Cara looked down at his bent head. 'I hope it gave
you a thrill,' she said. He finished punching out the
number and sat back in his regal chair with the
receiver at his ear. There were a few sparks in those
green eyes, but otherwise he seemed totally composed,
even with Valerie staring at his mussed hair, the red
mark on his jaw, the lipstick smudge.

'More guessing, Miss Matheson? Hope *what* gave
me a thrill?' He glanced at his secretary, who wore a

bland look as if trying to appear deaf as well as blind.

'Though I would have thought it was a trivial use of your power,' she continued scathingly.

He looked exasperated, both at his call which was apparently going unanswered, and at her. 'What was, Miss Matheson—*what*?'

'Having me sacked. You'll be able to sleep nights again knowing that you've saved all those trusting little Carrington's students from my subversive influence.'

Frowning, he leaned forward. 'I didn't——' he began to say as she went to the door. Then his call was answered and he barked something into the mouthpiece; his second phone rang and Valerie hurried forward to answer it. Cara left, giving the door a sharp, angry wrench behind her. It closed with a soft, sprung 'whssht-click'. The man was the ultimate in frustration. Even his doors wouldn't slam.

Danny and Pete were sympathetic, and furious at Mitchell Kirby. Danny gave her an odd look when she identified Holly's father as the escalator man.

'He's just the type to throw his weight around. I could tell just by looking at him. I don't know why you bothered being so friendly to him.'

'I wanted to make him smile,' she said drily.

They ate dinner and talked—Pete about his last modelling session for the sculpture class. 'A wasp flew in. I was a bit worried, I can tell you——' They talked about lessons—taking them as a student, giving them as a tutor. Danny had been teaching that day too, but as a volunteer. He was brilliant on piano as well as guitar and spent a few hours every week working with young handicapped people in rehabilitation centres.

'Until another job comes up, it's one way of earning

my dole money,' he always shrugged off his community spirit.

'The kid I was teaching today chucked her guitar at me,' he said, gingerly reaching over his shoulder. 'I think she drew blood. I'll get you to take a look at it later, Cara.'

'What did you do—give her one of *your* compositions to play?' Pete guffawed.

'Very funny. She was doing an old Bacharach number, in fact, and ended up screeching that I was a heartless monster expecting her to do things that a normal person can do. She was blinded in an accident a few months ago, poor kid.'

'Is it permanent?' asked Cara.

'Don't know yet.'

Cara made coffee and Pete took his cup into his own little Montmartre where he absently raised a ten-kilogram dumbbell in one hand while he studied his work. It wasn't unusual for Pete to do much of his daily workout at his easel. While he contemplated the development of his current painting, he developed the muscles appreciated by so many student sculptors. Lately Cara suspected that his contemplation might be divided between his art and his as yet unwritten marriage proposal to Viv.

'I'll get it,' he said when someone knocked at the door, for Cara was busy applying a plaster to the cut on Danny's back. Pete opened the door, a clutch of paintbrushes in one hand, a dumbbell in the other and his shirt open over a daubed chest. Cara looked to see if it was Miss Vernon come down to borrow something. But it wasn't their birdlike upstairs neighbour. It was Mitchell Kirby.

Cara drew in a sharp breath. What was he doing here? The man did a quick reconnaissance from the

uncleared dinner table to Pete's painting clutter, to his
partly bared chest and Danny's totally bared one. And
to Cara. Her hands slid from Danny's back. This was a
scene of debauchery to Mitchell Kirby, she supposed.
His *ménage à trois* to the life.

'May I come in, Miss Matheson?' he asked. An icy
front greeted him from Danny and Cara.

'Oh—you're a friend of Cara's?' Pete failed to pick
up the chill atmosphere and introduced himself,
casually tossing the dumbbell into his left hand with
the paintbrushes to shake the older man's hand.

'No. This is Kirby.' said Danny shortly.

'Well, well—is that right?' Pete's geniality van-
ished. He had a handshake of iron when he wanted,
and Cara suspected he was using it now. Mitchell
Kirby didn't seem as perturbed by the power of it so
much as the texture. He inspected his paint-smudged
palm when Pete let go.

'May I?' he said, and plucked up the disreputable
rag that dangled from Pete's pocket to wipe off the
transferred paint.

'Just why have you come here, Mr Kirby? I really
thought we'd said everything,' said Cara.

'You may have said everything, but I haven't. Can
we talk privately?' He tossed the paint-rag to Pete and
looked around rather unhopefully at the crammed
premises, noting the posters, the plants, the collage,
the paintings.

'No.'

'Don't mind us,' said Pete, ostentatiously courteous.
'We'll make like we're not here, won't we, Danny?'

'Oh sure,' Danny agreed.

Mitchell Kirby's mouth tightened. 'All right. I came
because——' he paused and cleared his throat. Pete's
outsized brush bristled audibly across his canvas. He

looked up at the unlit fluorescent light and muttered a few uncomplimentary words about Mr Parini's lighting. Danny looked up too as he shrugged into his shirt.

'Thar she blows,' he said from long habit. Mitchell Kirby's gaze was drawn irresistibly to the ceiling.

'*Ya-hoo*!' sneezed Miss Vernon upstairs. Another two '*Ya-hoos* followed in quick succession.

'It's rodeo time tonight, pardners,' Pete joked.

'*Ya-hoo-oo*!' The rogue light came on as if prompted by Miss Vernon's sneeze. It smouldered and flickered.

'Good on you, Miss Vernon!' Pete called up to the ceiling, then catching Kirby's baffled eye said, 'Upstairs neighbour. Hay fever.'

Cara took no notice of all this. 'Yes, Mr Kirby—you've come because——?' she prompted as if there had been no interruption.

'I have to——'

'*Ya-hoo*!' Miss Vernon was getting louder. The fluorescent light stuttered prematurely from smouldering to strobe effects. 'It's about your——' he began again, eyes wandering to Danny who had his shirt buttoned now and was twisting gymnastically trying to look over his shoulder.

'Is there any blood on my shirt, Cara?' he asked.

'Hardly any,' she said perfunctorily, and to Kirby, 'Well—you were saying?'

Danny looked sulky at his dismissal. He took the bouzouki off the wall and, sitting, began quietly to pluck out 'Never on Sunday'.

'Miss Matheson, there seems to have been some——' Mitchell Kirby said. Twang—twang—Pete absently stretched a chest expander while he looked at his painting. Softly he began to sing along with Danny's bouzouki. Miss Vernon sneezed. '*Ya-hoo*!' '—call me on a Monday, a Monday a——' The bouzouki grew louder, faster.

'Mr Kirby,' said Cara, putting her hands on her hips, 'I *wish* you'd stop waffling and say why you're here!'

He glared at her. 'Waffling? My God, I can't even hear myself think in this madhouse!' He seized her arm and strode to the door. Cara was towed along, too startled at his sudden aggression to do anything else. At the door he ignored her protests and, taking her by the arms, deposited her outside. The bouzouki music stopped suddenly.

'I'll bring her back,' he informed the boys, who had bristled to attention. 'I'm a lawyer, not Jack the Ripper.'

'Come,' he ordered as he shut the door and whisked her across the concrete 'lawn' to a grey Peugeot. He swung the door open. 'Get in.'

'Why should I?'

'Because it's raining?' he suggested, holding out a hand to the light sprinkle falling, 'And because it's quiet in there,' he said, enunciating with crisp exaggeration. 'Very—very—quiet.' A stray sneeze yelped out from upstairs.

'—but never, ever on a Sunday, a Sunday——' Mitchell Kirby closed his eyes for a second. 'Get in. I want to talk to you. Please.'

The car was spacious, luxurious. Cara gaped. 'You've got a phone in your car!'

'It isn't exactly unheard of,' he muttered, getting in and slotting his key into the ignition. The engine turned over with an expensive purr. Windscreen wipers suavely swished away the raindrop sparkle. Cara swivelled in her seat.

'Now look—I don't want to go anywhere with you,' she told him.

'Likewise. But with a bit of luck we might find some neutral ground somewhere suitable for an apology.'

'Ha!' she cried. 'So you *do* have a conscience!' Then, in tones of awe, 'Are you actually going to apologise to me?'

'No,' he said silkily. '*You* are going to apologise to *me*.'

'Me?' she squeaked. 'What do I have to apologise for—*I'm* the one without a job—*I'm* the one who——'

'Not while I'm driving, Miss Matheson,' he said wearily. 'I've had a long day—all the legal joys of a multi-national and a Japanese consortium, and I had to eat lunch with a very rich, very loud, very rude client.' He took his hand from the wheel and rubbed at his midriff.

'Indigestion?' she asked, and he threw her a grim look. 'You shouldn't eat with people you dislike—it plays havoc with your digestive system.'

'We don't all have the freedom of choice allowed music teachers and buskers,' he pointed out.

'Ex-music teacher,' she interpolated smartly. Another grim look.

'There was nothing wrong with my digestion until *you* burst into my office and broke an emotional storm over my head!'

'Good,' she said with satisfaction, 'I'm glad I've made you suffer a little bit.'

'Oh, you have,' he murmured, and pulled in to the kerb outside a tiny restaurant-cum-coffee shop. 'And I have a feeling the suffering isn't over yet.'

They went inside. He ordered coffee with an unconsciously lofty air. Cara reckoned they would get the quickest service in town, so impressed did the waitress seem. She stared a bit at Cara—at her pink blouse split along the shoulder and tied here and there, at her turquoise skirt and her hair which was braided from a topknot. The waitress clearly thought her an unlikely companion for Mitchell Kirby. The girl hurried off without actually curtseying and Cara looked at Mitchell Kirby across a tiny round table.

'Do you always live in such chaos?' he asked.

'What chaos?'

He gave a snort. 'Enough said. Why should there be blood on his shirt?'

'Never mind that. What am I supposed to apologise for—always bearing in mind that I am now unemployed because of your nineteenth-century scruples? I hope you're paying for the coffee,' she finished.

He sighed. 'I undertake to pay for the coffee. And let's get something straight right now, shall we? I did not—repeat, did not have you sacked from Carrington's.'

She stared at him. 'Just a coincidence then—right? You put me on the cross-examination stand at the soirée, found out all the reprehensible details of my past, present and future, and bingo! I'm out of a job at the very place where you happen to be a director.'

'It's true that I asked Strachan to assign another teacher to Holly. I made it crystal clear to him that I had no cause for complaint regarding your professional competence. I—intimated that Holly was a difficult student and that a—different teacher personality might work out more beneficially. That's all.'

Cara studied him intently. There was a directness in his green eyes, a ring of conviction in his voice. She believed him. 'All right. Why did I lose my job, then?'

'I've spoken to Strachan——'

'Spoken to him—when?'

'After you left my office—this would go much quicker if you didn't interrupt——' he said. The coffee arrived, delivered reverently by the waitress. Mitchell Kirby nodded his thanks. 'It seems that Strachan over-reacted. He is—how can I put it—anxious to please anyone on the board.'

'Obsequious,' she put in. 'I think that's the word you want. Sorry,' she added as he frowned at the interruption.

'He construed my request as a criticism of you and decided it might gain favour with me to—fire you. I suspect he already had a few reservations about you which made the decision an easy one for him.'

Cara nodded. 'Well, I apologise for accusing you wrongly. I did rather jump to conclusions. I don't usually. It was probably because I was so hurt about you taking Holly away from me.'

Silence. Mitchell Kirby sipped at his coffee, eyed her over the *cappuccino* foam.

'Hurt?' he queried.

'I'm very fond of Holly.'

'Not many of her teachers are.'

'She's not everyone's idea of a cute teenager,' she agreed, 'but sometimes she lets me in, and what I've seen I've liked.'

He was quiet for a long time. 'Lets you in,' he repeated, looking down at the table. 'I've probably done a very stupid thing.'

'Fathers do stupid things all the time. Mine did.'

He looked up at her. 'Is that supposed to be a comfort to me, Miss Matheson?'

She laughed. 'Holly won't necessarily turn out like me just because she's rebellious now—though she might enjoy life a lot more if she took my road instead of yours——'

'Let's not go into that,' he said heavily.

Cara gazed up at the ceiling. '—of course, she'd run

the risk of being labelled a "cheap little itinerant".'

He winced. 'I was fighting mad when I said that. I'd apologise if you hadn't already had your revenge.' He rubbed his jaw and she grinned.

'So I did.'

He fell silent, deep in thought. 'Holly doesn't even "let *me* in" lately,' he said at last. 'Apart from a few girlfriends I don't think she communicates with anyone much. She's at that awkward age when she needs a mother——'

'You could provide her with one.'

'It isn't something you can come up with like a pair of roller skates,' he pointed out drily.

'What about Cleo?'

He stiffened a bit. 'Cleo is an old family friend. She was very close to my wife.' He toyed with his spoon. 'What—what things did Holly talk to you about?' he asked.

'Um—look if you're trying to ask me my impressions, here they are—she feels plain and uninteresting, not uncommon at that age. She's jealous of your work and of Cleo and thinks you might be considering marrying again and isn't sure of her place in your life. And she worries over little things—her hair, for instance——'

'Her hair?'

'She asked me if she should have it cropped short.'

'And you advised her?' His eyes went to her wisping topknot and the braid which was wound around Indian fashion with a leather thong.

'Sure. I told her it would look great in a cute punk cut, bleached on top and maybe just a tiny shaved strip along each side——" Cara demonstrated with her hands.

'What?' he bellowed. The other diners looked over.

Cara threw back her head and laughed.

'I was kidding. But what would it matter? She's young and she wants to experiment.'

'Oh God!' he stared at her, aghast. 'A punk cut—bleached?'

'Relax. Punk isn't so trendy any more. But if you want her to leave it the way it is, tell her you like it that way.'

'I do tell her. At least, she knows I like it—dammit,' he said defensively at Cara's disbelieving look, 'I'm a man. I don't always think to tell her about her hair. I'm so busy.'

'Get your watch to remind you,' she suggested. 'Set that neat little alarm—beep, beep—time to compliment Holly on her hair.'

He iced over. 'Not amusing. I'm well aware that I don't always handle Holly with tact. If you were a parent you might realise that tact doesn't always come easily when you're under other pressures and tired and your child tries her damnedest to be provocative and likes all the wrong TV programmes and takes up with friends who smoke and drink—'

'And influence her—like the one she ran away with?' she said, seeing how much he cared. 'Yes, I see—I apologise.'

Silence. The foam on the *cappuccinos* slipped to the half-way mark.

'I've arranged for you to have your job back,' he said.

Cara nearly choked on her coffee. 'You have?'

'Just one small problem. In a fit of efficiency, Strachan hired a temporary teacher for the next two weeks. Are you willing to wait until then to go back?'

She nodded. Mr Strachan would be thoroughly confused. To please this man he'd fired her, and now to please him he was taking her back. She was moved that Mitchell Kirby had made the effort on her behalf. He was a busy man and he could have simply shrugged off her dismissal. 'Thank you,' she said.

'Don't mention it,' he replied drily, 'I got a real thrill out of wielding my power on a trivial matter.'

She laughed, then stopped as he winced and rubbed at his stomach.

'Have you eaten since lunch, Mitch?' His name slipped out easily, familiarly as if she'd been saying it for ages. She didn't even know if people called him Mitch. Maybe Mitchell. But Mitch felt right. He blinked a few times.

'No.'

'Then you should have a snack.'

'I don't want a snack.'

'Your digestive juices are probably attacking the walls of your stomach.' Cara waved a hand at the waitress and the girl brought a menu. 'Wait, we'll order now. Lasagne,' she read out to Mitch. 'Too spicy, probably—moussaka. Moussaka?' She lifted a brow at him.

'I told you, I don't want——'

'Omelette,' she said, closing the menu with a snap. 'Even a tired professional stomach can deal with that.'

Mitch looked at the waitress. 'I don't want anything.'

'A cheese omelette,' Cara overruled him with a grin. 'He's very indecisive. Something to drink?' she asked him. Bemused and amused, he leaned back in his chair.

'Milk?' he said in mock meekness.

'No—too much cholesterol at your age. Mineral water. I'll have the lasagne,' she tagged on as the girl moved away. 'All this talk of food has made me hungry,' she explained to Mitch. 'I couldn't eat properly earlier tonight, worrying about finding another job.'

'I'm so happy to have revived your appetite,' he said and there was a funny look in his eyes—a look of speculation, and keen interest, and warmth.

They raised their coffee cups as if by mutual consent. After a few seconds Mitch put his cup down suddenly.

'Why *was* there blood on his shirt?'

'His student threw her guitar at him.'

'Well, of course, why didn't I think of that?' he murmured.

Cara laughed and explained about Danny's voluntary piano and guitar teaching at the rehab centres. Mitch looked thoughtful at that.

'He turned around to get another piece of music and she threw her guitar at him. It could have been much worse, of course,' she said, rolling her eyes, 'it could have been one of his *piano* students he upset.'

Mitch chuckled. He tilted his head back and laughed.

Cara clutched at the table as if to steady herself. 'Good lord,' she said in a stage whisper, 'I did it!'

'Did what?'

'Got you to smile.'

He did it again, and Cara liked it. She liked it a lot. His smile moved his face about, re-aligned the rather lean cheeks, cut nice creases into them. It tipped up his eyes at the corners and made his mouth quite amazingly boyish.

'You know, for a while there I wondered if you had teeth. I never glimpsed them,' she confided, trying to ignore the door-knocker rhythm of her heart. He chuckled again. The man didn't seem able to stop now that he'd started.

'And now that you've seen them, what do you think?'

She pretended to consider. 'I like them. They're very straight—did you have braces as a boy?'

He shook his head as if incredulous to find himself talking about it, and told her about his two years in braces and the accompanying agonies with bugle lessons, and Cara related her similar difficulties with braces and flute lessons, and eventually the food came and music piped softly in the background as they talked about other music they had loved and hated as children and the effect it had on their parents.

'Mine still wince when they see a military movie and hear all those calls. They agree the Last Post was the worst, though. I used to play it every Anzac Day at school. What about your folks?'

'Oh—the only thing my folks ever agreed on was that I should have braces,' she said lightly and set to on her lasagne. In spite of his earlier resistance, Mitchell attacked his omelette with gusto. Finishing it, he set down his cutlery with an air of surprise, drank some mineral water and watched her finish her food.

'You know,' he said reflectively, rubbing a hand over his midriff, 'I think you're right. You should never eat with someone you dislike.'

Cara's heart dropped. 'Don't tell me—you've got excruciating indigestion again,' she said flippantly.

Mitchell held her gaze, eyes warm and smiling. 'Not a trace,' he said softly. She felt a surge of elation—she hadn't felt like this since she had fallen crazily for Guy. He likes me, she thought, hugging the knowledge close. She actually blushed. In the restaurant's dim light he wouldn't notice.

'Cara——' he said slowly, letting her name roll off his tongue as if he was tasting it. 'I'd like to——' he mulled a bit, took a sip of mineral water. 'I've been invited to a party . . . would you come with me?'

She smiled to hide her confusion. 'This is so sudden, Mitch—one minute I'm a possible bad influence on your daughter and the next you ask me for a date!'

He smiled. 'I told you—I'm too old, my views too formed to be in danger of subversion.' That was his first mistake. He had hinted as much, but she would have liked him to say that he no longer considered her a bad influence on Holly.

'Well—thanks a lot, but I don't think so.'

'Why not?'

'Oh—I'd probably be bored.'

'Bored!' he exclaimed. Heads turned towards him and he leaned over, green eyes snapping, and lowered his voice. 'Bored? How can you assume that?'

'Anyway, if I said yes, what would I wear that you'd want to be seen with? I don't have to be told that you hate my clothes. I don't even have a pair of high-heeled shoes now that I wrecked my heel on your pavement. I'd look like a gypsy and you aren't the kind of man to be seen with a gypsy.'

He didn't deny it. His second mistake.

'You could—buy something, couldn't you?' he said.

Cara stared at him. 'You—arrogant, supercilious—snob!' She flung her crumpled napkin at him and got up. 'Don't bother about driving me home. I'd rather walk.'

Minutes later he caught up with her in the street. In the rain. He grabbed her arm, whizzed her about.

'What the hell's the matter with you?' he demanded.

'Buy something! *Buy* something, he says, and then asks what's the matter. I wear what I want to wear because I'm me, not a store mannequin to be tricked out in suitable clothing so as not to cause embarrassment.'

'Good God, is that all?' he said, astonished. 'Women do buy party clothes, Cara—most *like* buying party clothes. It seemed a sensible suggestion——'

'Oh, *sensible*,' she mocked.

'Look—why don't we move out of the rain?' He pulled her and she dug in her heels and resisted.

'I don't want to move out of the rain. I like the rain—but then I'm not sensible! I cringe to think what this party would be like with sensible you and your sensible friends—actually I'm surprised you'd even consider going to a party! Look at you!' She curled her lip at his damp but ultra-neat clothes. 'Practically a store dummy.' She flicked his tie. 'Don't you ever loosen up a bit?' Before she could stop herself she was at the knot of the tie, tugging it loose from his collar. Mitchell Kirby looked down in astonishment at her hands on his clothes. The tie hung askew and she fumbled with the top button of his shirt.

'I must be crazy!' he said. 'Asking you to go any-where with me. Look at you—sandals from Ancient Rome and—and peepholes in your clothes——' He plucked at her sleeves and some ties came undone along the split shoulders; his fingers slid through the openings just as Cara triumphantly pushed open his shirt collar.

'There!' she said, looking up into his face. She was suddenly still. So was he. Everything stopped, or so it seemed. Oh, out somewhere else, way, way off—car tyres swished along a wet road and feet scurried, hurried over pavement puddles. Rain slanted down, gurgled into drains, dripped from shining leaves and shadowed eaves. The incomparable smell of warm, wet streets and earth was in the air, and the warm, masculine scent of the man holding her. Cara felt the rain cold and spiky on her cheek, Mitch's skin warm beneath her hands—his hands warm on her shoulders.

They moved together—he bent to her, she craned to him. Their mouths met in a first, tentative touch—a delicate sampling of something new. Touch and retreat and touch again. Their lips parted, re-shaped. Raindrops ran down between them and they tasted them, clean and sweet, and Mitch gathered her up in a great bearhug and Cara wound her arms around his neck and their kiss gathered force with the rain.

They drew apart—gulped air, stared at each other.

'I'll take you home,' he said huskily. In silence they walked back to the car. In silence he started it, pulled away from the kerb. Cara looked out of the window at the shining pavements and the rain's slanting silver-point in street-light haloes. Where were they headed? she wondered, lightly touching her fingers to her lips.

The car telephone beeped. Mitch picked up the receiver and embarked on a business discussion which lasted the short journey home. In fact he was still speaking to his caller when he braked outside her flat. She leapt out into the rain.

'Don't interrupt your call. Good night, Mitch.'

She paused at the door to see him drive off, talking into the phone. Where were they headed? she asked herself again derisively. In opposite directions.

CHAPTER FOUR

CARA was at a loose end on Friday. She cleaned the flat, washed her car, then on impulse drove up to Mount Glorious and sat a long time looking out over the Samford Valley thinking that perhaps, after Christmas, she might move on. Somewhere new. The longest she'd ever stayed anywhere, apart from the long, dreary years of childhood at home, had been that year in Paris with Guy. Over the years she had accumulated hordes of friends. She could go almost anywhere and find a good friend. It was how she always found her accommodation. Her friends gave her letters of introduction to theirs and they became her friends and then when she had the urge to move on again, she took introductions to friends of a friend in another city, another town. It was the way she had met Pete and Danny.

Cross-legged, she sat on the mountain top and played her flute until the cool, pure notes brought the tranquillity of meditation. Then she drove home again. A northern town would be nice for a change, she thought, looking around at her posters and her pot plants and her collage. Cairns. She went to look at a note pinned up on the untidy notice board. A teacher at Carrington's had given her some names and an address in Cairns. She already had somewhere to go, people to share accommodation with. Yes, Cairns. The beaches were good up there and there were plenty of jobs in the tourist season. So after Christmas she would move on. Cara was conscious that this time the

decision was being made cold. She felt no urge to
leave; none at all. She didn't want to think about that.
Shaking her head she met the unflinching stare of the
Boobook Owl. Cara pulled a face at it. 'Oh, what do
you know?' she muttered.

The Mall was busy that night.

'A forty-fiver, do you reckon?' Danny grinned,
looking at their proceeds after an hour.

'Possibly,' murmured Cara. She was absent, watching out for Mitch like some besotted teenager.

'So what happened last night?' asked Danny. Last
night when she'd returned, Danny had gone out with a
musician friend. 'With you and Kirby.'

'I got him to smile,' she said, then catching Danny's
arrested gaze, added, 'and I'll have my job back in two
weeks. It was a misunderstanding—all Strachan's
idea. Mitch is fixing up my reinstatement.'

'So it's "Mitch", is it?' He gave a slow whistle but
said nothing more.

Holly stopped by and demanded her favourite pop
song from Danny. Had the embargo been lifted, then?
Cara wondered. The buskers no longer out of bounds
to Mitch's daughter? The girl wore her school uniform
and had her hair clipped back with big, neon-pink
plastic bulldog clips.

'Does the school allow you to wear those Molly clips
with uniform?' Cara asked in a break.

'Course not.' Holly tossed her head, tried to look
tough. 'I'll get a detention if a prefect sees me. But I
don't care. I'm sick of looking like Little Goody Two
Shoes.'

'Haven't you asked your dad yet about having your
hair cut?'

'I might ask him tonight. We're having dinner in
town, Dad and me.' There was a quickly repressed

eagerness about her glance over at the glass doors. It was, Cara thought, an encouraging sign that Holly, though resentful and rebellious, didn't simply go out and have her hair done without waiting for permission. Her father's opinion mattered to her, and she clearly relished the idea of being with him. All was not lost. Now that she knew Mitch a little better, Cara wondered how things had ever reached such a pass between him and his daughter.

'I'm sorry to hear that you had to give up Tuesday lessons,' she said, wondering what Mitch had told the girl about the changes.

'Oh, come on, Cara. Dad tried to pretend he was changing my lessons to a Wednesday because it was more convenient for Mrs Leslie to pick me up from Carrington's. She's our housekeeper. But I'll bet he just wanted to get me away from you. He probably thinks you'd be a bad influence on me because you're—well, different, know what I mean?' Holly paused. 'And he's frightened, I guess.'

'That you might run away again?'

She was startled, demanding to know how Cara had found out about that. Her eyes rounded when she heard that her father and Cara had talked the night before.

'So *that's* why he was late home,' she said, brightening. 'I thought he must have been with *Cleo*.'

'Didn't he say where he'd been?'

'Oh, he never tells me *anything*,' Holly said dramatically. Maybe she didn't want to listen. The house was large enough for evasion. And there were ways of cutting oneself off from parents even in a small house. Cara sighed. She herself had learned them all from necessity long before she'd reached Holly's age. Holly, on the other hand, might simply be indulging in some teenage martyrdom. It was fashionable to be misunderstood by parents. The girl looked up as Mitch emerged from the Southdown Building; the flash of eagerness on her face disappeared as an ash-blonde woman appeared with him.

'Oh—it's *her*,' Holly muttered in disappointment. '*Cleo*.'

She was in her thirties—not beautiful or handsome, but a woman who made very intelligent use of her assets. She was immaculately groomed, and wore a deep red two-piece outfit with great panache. Cara could easily see her playing hostess at the big white house with its cage of exotic birds and its peacock shrieking on the lawns.

Mitch greeted his daughter, then looked at Cara. 'Hello, Cara,' he said coolly, composedly as if he'd never kissed her in the rain the night before—or asked her to go to a party with him. In retrospect that impulse must seem as foolhardy to him as it did to her. She was grateful he was backing off, Cara told herself. She didn't want to get involved with Mitch.

He introduced Cleo, who was absently warm and charming as if her mind was elsewhere but her manners were operating on automatic. 'Hello—having a good night?' she said, looking at the coins in the guitar case. She flipped open her bag, found a coin and smilingly tossed it in with the others. As she hadn't heard any of their music, the gesture smacked of charity, though Cara knew it was not meant that way. Her smile was stiff. She could see what Holly meant about Cleo. Already she felt irritated with her and guilty about it.

'Why, Holly, what have you done to your hair?' Cleo said fondly, 'it looks so much prettier the old way——' So saying, she hitched her soft leather bag

under her arm and plucked the two neon clips from
Holly's hair with a magician's '*Voilà*' gesture. The
girl's hair fell silkily around her face. 'There, that's
much better.' Cleo winked confidentially at her
goddaughter. 'You don't need these novelty orna-
ments—you look so sweet with the simple, classic
style.'

Wrong, wrong! Cara thought, closing her eyes. You
silly woman—— They started to move away. Holly
looked back at Cara as if to say, 'Didn't I tell you so?';
Mitch gave a mere nod as good night. The three of
them walked away to disappear among the potted
palms and the pottering people.

Cara and Danny splurged on coffee at Jimmie's in
the Mall that night, then went home. Cara kept on
thinking about Mitch. Crazy. All she'd wanted to do
was see him smile, and she almost wished she'd let him
pass on by and then she'd never have known. Known
what? The question hung there, unanswered in her
mind. She met the knowing stare of the owl on her
poster and stirred uncomfortably in her chair.

'That thing will have to go,' she said as Pete sat
chewing his pen over a letter to Viv and Danny
hunched over the guitar and notation for a new song.
'I can't stand its know-it-all look.'

'Well, now you know why its an endangered
species,' said Pete.

Endangered species? There could be another of
them to add to the list, thought Cara when she opened
the front door on Saturday morning and gaped at the
spectacle that awaited her. It was Holly, slim as a reed
in cotton pants and a candy-striped sleeveless sweater
of such vibrant colour that it might have attracted
attention had it not been for her hair. What was left of
her hair.

It had been shaved so close to her head at the sides and back that her scalp showed through. There was a thicket of formerly lustrous dark brown hair left on top, but gelled now and spiked up and out, like the bristles of a worn scrubbing brush. Cara clamped down on her immediate reactions. Holly stood there looking defiant and proud and scared to death, and it was clear she was here for moral support.

'Oh,' Cara said, and smiled. 'You've had your hair cut.' It had to be the understatement of the year. She heard Pete come in from the back door and turned around, giving him a meaningful stare. 'Holly's had her hair cut—you know Holly, don't you, Pete?' She should have known her warning was unnecessary. Pete's fellow art students were an adventurous lot, and he didn't even raise an eyebrow at Holly's shorn, worn brush style.

'Sure. Hi, kid—changing your image, huh? Want a Coke?'

Holly relaxed visibly. She smiled, came inside and looked around with interest—had a can of Coke and became quite expansive. But Cara couldn't allow her to slip into a false sense of security.

'Does your father know you were going to the hairdresser today?' she probed. Holly's grin snapped in like a rubber band. She ran a hand over the back of her neck. The friction must be tremendous, Cara thought.

'No,' she admitted. 'He won't like it, but who cares?'

Well, it was pretty obvious that she did, and that she was putting off the moment of truth. Mitch was supposed to pick her up in town in an hour, Holly said, but she'd hopped on a bus and come out here just to show Cara. She wandered around looking at Pete's paintings, abruptly turned away from the Boobook owl, caught a glimpse of herself in a mirror and swallowed hard. Cara cursed silently. Damn Cleo! The silly woman had practically challenged the girl to do something drastic. 'So sweet with the simple, classic style'! What rebellious teenage girl wouldn't want to change *that*?

'Why don't I drive you home, Holly?' said Cara, and the girl whirled about.

'Would you?' She masked her relief and added casually, 'Oh sure, that would be great, Cara.' She phoned her father to tell him she was on her way home and with whom. 'Oh—I—just bumped into her——' she said with a guilty glance at Cara.

During the drive she kept up a steady, nervous chatter. School was *boring* and her grandparents had flown to New York for an international conference on law. Grandpa was Justice Holley, it turned out. 'I was named after Mum's family.' She talked about her mother then, almost compulsively, touching her hair as if cutting it had somehow triggered off memories. Maybe she was wondering what her mother would have thought of it. 'She was very clever. Cleo went to school with her. She always says that Mum had everything—beauty, brains and background. Did I tell you that she was a famous barrister? She was better known than Dad even. Everyone said she would have been a Q.C. if ... She was always busy with cases. Did I tell you she was killed in a plane crash?'

'Yes, you told me that, Holly.' A light aircraft chartered to take her and a client out west had crashed on take-off.

'She was expecting a baby when she died.'

'Oh, no!' said Cara, surprised and saddened, 'I'm so sorry. It must have been a double sadness for you, losing a brother or sister too——'

'Oh—she wouldn't have had the baby,' the girl said, turning her head to stare out the window. 'It would have interfered with her career. She probably wouldn't have had me, but I suppose she left it too late to—you know.'

Cara was appalled. 'Holly, how can you possibly know such a thing? I'm sure you're wrong.'

The girlish green eyes were suddenly old with the weary wisdom of the young. 'I know. I have it from an unimpeachable source. See——' she added with a fake laugh, 'I'm beginning to sound like her and Dad. Maybe I'll end up a lawyer yet.'

She fell silent as they approached the gateway of her home. Never said a word when Cara drove in, swerving to miss the peacock which made a gawky dash from shrubbery on to the driveway. The grey Peugeot was parked outside the garages. A man was washing it. Cara turned off the ignition and sat there with Holly for a moment.

'Do you want me to come in with you?' she asked, wondering what she was doing getting involved in a domestic fracas.

'If you like,' said Holly, ultra-casual. They got out of the Mini and Holly waved to the man washing the car. 'Hi, Mr Welland.'

Mr Welland froze. His sponge gave a great involuntary heave, releasing a gout of white foam over the Peugeot's windscreen.

'Why don't I just—go on ahead——' Cara suggested tactfully. 'I want to—er—have a word with your father about—um——'

Mitch came to answer her knock at the graceful sliding doors that gave accesse to the vine-covered patio. He wore shorts and sandshoes and a shirt that

was open half-way down his chest, and she was
diverted from her purpose. He was impressively hairy.
His legs were lean and muscular and his chest was
really rather marvellous——

'As I knew you were coming, I left the buttons
undone,' he said drily, and she whipped her eyes from
his chest to his face, conscious of a slow burn in her
cheeks and a quick tempo change in her pulse rate.
For once she hadn't anything to say.

'Why, Miss Matheson, I do believe I've embarrassed you. I didn't think it was possible.' His green
eyes gleamed satisfaction. A smile tugged at his
mouth. Darn it, she shouldn't have come here—it was
no business of hers to act as buffer between father and
daughter. Not when the father looked like this. She
felt in dire danger—wanted to take off down his drive
in her Mini.

'No, no. It's just such a surprise to see you without a
suit,' she said with a very creditable smile. 'I thought
you'd been grafted into a grey suit.' Her eyes went to
his wrist. He still wore Superwatch, she noticed.
'Mitch——'

He looked over her shoulder. 'Where's Holly?'

'She's talking to Mr Welland.' If Mr Welland hadn't
keeled over by now.

'Like a drink, Cara?' He took her elbow and guided
her inside to the massive living-room. 'Coffee—
mineral water——?'

'Mineral water, thanks. I—er—Mitch, you remember we were talking about Holly's hair on
Thursday——'

'I remember.' He bent to take a bottle from the bar
fridge. 'You had your little joke about a punk cut with
bleached top and shaved strips.'

Cara didn't want him to remember *that* well. 'Oh

yes, well, that's ridiculous, of course. I mean bleached would be just too much——' she gave a tinny laugh. 'But of course, you know girls like to experiment——'

'Yes, so I've noticed.' He looked at her unruly mane. 'I've nothing against that, within reason.' With his back to her he lifted the top off the mineral water and poured some.

'Holly is—has been—very bored with her hair——'

He turned his head slowly. 'Has been?'

'She went to the hairdresser this morning——'

His eyes went to the empty doorway. 'And?'

'Well—she had her hair cut.'

'Cut?' he echoed.

'Short.'

'Short?' He came over carrying the drinks. 'How short?'

Cara reached out for her glass, took a gulp from it.

'Quite short,' she said.

It was as well he had relinquished the drink into her hand, for he caught sight of Holly just then and it meant only one glass fell to the floor. It sloshed mineral water over his feet and rolled to and fro on the carpet.

'Bloody hell!' he whispered.

'Don't be angry with her,' Cara implored in a low voice. 'She's already having doubts about it herself, and she——'

He turned on her with an icy glare. She needn't have worried that he would vent his fury on Holly. Oh, no. He didn't blame Holly at all.

'What is this? A collaboration? No, it's *your* doing, isn't it? You encouraged her, didn't you? Knowing how I felt about it, you deliberately incited my daughter to go and make herself look like a—a——' he looked at his daughter and closed his eyes momentarily. 'Bloody *hell*!'

Cara nearly choked at the unfairness of this, but said nothing. Maybe it wouldn't hurt if she drew some fire from Holly until he got over the initial shock.

'I decided all by myself!' Holly informed him. 'It's *my* decision to look like this and I *like* it! I don't know why you have to drop your glass over it. Cara and Pete didn't think it was anything to get excited about.'

'Cara and Pete wouldn't!' he hooted. 'Cara and Pete are quite at home with freaks!' He looked as if he regretted saying that the moment it was out, but was too angry to retract.

'Well, I wouldn't mind being at home with them too,' Holly blurted out tearfully. 'I don't seem to belong *here*!'

'Holly, come back here——' roared Mitch as she flounced away. 'Holly——' The girl took off for the stairs, bolted up them two at a time, ignoring him. A moment later came the slam of a door. Mitch's head jerked at the sound. He turned to Cara.

'Satisfied?' he gritted, catching her arm and swinging her close. 'Is your tiny anti-establishment mind happy now that you've managed to turn my daughter into something from a—a street gang?'

Cara's temper flared. 'What's the matter, Mitch? Will you be ashamed to be seen with her now that she fails to conform to your standards? Is important, successful Mr Kirby afraid of what people might think if his little girl displays some individuality?'

'Individuality?' he expostulated. 'She looks like somebody's discarded toothbrush!'

'Well, maybe she looks like that because she feels like somebody's discarded *daughter*!' Cara snapped back, thrusting her face up to his. He looked fit to kill at that and she tried to pull away. But he dragged her closer still, glaring down at her. Through the folds of her thin skirt Cara felt the pressure of his legs against hers.

'I *knew* it, the first time I saw you,' he said between his teeth. 'On the escalator I got this feeling—trouble, I thought. And hell, was I right! You've got my daughter looking like a hoodlum and you've got me——' He bit down on the words and pushed her away, then shoved his hands into his back pockets as if he didn't trust them on the loose. Abruptly he turned on his heel and strode away, up the curved staircase where Holly had gone.

Cara tried not to think about it. She drove out to the bay the next day, sat a lonely distance from Sunday picnickers and played her flute. He *had* remembered her on the escalator after all. She couldn't repress a certain satisfaction at that. 'You've got my daughter looking like a hoodlum and you've got me——' Doing what? What had she done to Mitch?

Driven him to distraction by the look of it. Cara saw him on Monday in the most unlikely place. Having confided that morning to Mario Vella, the local greengrocer, that she was temporarily out of a job, she had been crushed to that ample gentleman's bosom.

'You work for me today, uh? My Angela, she can't come to work—I pay you and you take home the bruised fruit for the fruit salad too, uh?' With these inducements Cara accepted the large calico apron usually filled by Mario's large Angela and started arranging fruit while her boss burst into a Verdi aria out the back over his sacks of potatoes and cabbages. Just after lunch she propped herself against the counter and yawned over the pyramid of persimmons she was constructing.

'Going to juggle them?' said a familiar, sarcastic voice.

She spun around, two persimmons in one hand, three in the other.

'Oh! What are you doing here?'

'Well, I'm not buying any fruit,' he snapped, and she flinched back from a blaze of anger.

'How did you know I was here?' she asked, struck by the fascinating contrast of Mitch in creaseless grey superfine and pale blue shirt against the luscious red and gold of the persimmons.

'I called at the flat and Danny told me.' He stood there staring down at her, his mouth working a bit.

'Well?' she prompted when he produced nothing from his suppressed well of words. 'What is it, Mitch? Have you looked me up to blame me again for Holly's new hairdo, because if so I can tell you——'

'Holly has been suspended from school.'

'Oh, dear.'

'Oh, dear?' he repeated. 'Is that all you can say?'

'Was it because of her hair?'

'Of course it was because of her hair. *Everything* seems to be because of her hair! Suddenly hair is dominating my Life!'

'Don't shout. It isn't the end of the world. Where is Holly?'

'She's outside in the car.' He took a deep breath. 'When she was suspended,' he went on, punching out each word, 'some interfering, militant, rebel fellow-student who must be a lot like you phoned an evening newspaper——'

'Oh-oh!' muttered Cara.

'A reporter spoke to her. A photographer took her picture. The story has gone to press.'

Mitch took a turn around the fruit shop, kicking

away a discarded lettuce leaf, a fallen potato, with the toe of one impeccable shoe. The potato skittered across the floor.

'Well, I'm sorry, but I don't know what I'm supposed to——'

He stopped by a mound of melons and pointed at her.

'It's all your fault.'

Cara set her hands on her hips. 'It is *not*. She did her own thing, and anyway the hair will grow again——'

'Well now, I'm glad you mentioned that,' he said softly, silkily, and Cara tensed at the abrupt change. 'Her school might take her back after a week's growth—or it could take two weeks, and in the meantime I have to find someone to stay at the house with her while she's exiled at home. Our housekeeper might normally do it, but Mrs Leslie has a new grandchild and is unavailable. Holly's grandparents have just gone away—my parents are in Adelaide— which leaves one logical person.'

'Cleo?' she grimaced.

'You.'

She argued, of course, with great feeling. Mario, still singing, popped out to discover with delighted surprise that two Australians were engaged in a verbal battle worthy of his ancestors. He disappeared again and his resonant tenor soared like a descant over their voices.

It was a ridiculous idea, Cara scoffed. An excellent one, he said—she had no work for two weeks and he would pay her, naturally. Oh, naturally!

If he thought she was responsible for Holly's hairdo, and she wasn't—didn't he think she was just the wrong person to have looking after her? Oh, but he just *knew* Cara would be a model of decorum, if she really did want her job back at Carrington's.

'That's blackmail!' she protested.

'Don't be damned stupid,' he snorted. 'Of course it isn't blackmail. But if you led Holly off on some other idiotic prank you don't think in all conscience I could stand by my recommendation to Strachan, do you?'

'How would it look to people, do you think?' she demanded. 'You and me in the same house.'

'You and me and Holly,' he reminded her. 'If I'm not concerned I don't see why you should be. You already live with two men.'

'But that's diff——' she started to say, and bit it off, not wanting to think about just how different it was.

'Let's go. I need you now—I have to get back to work. How long will it take you to pack?'

'For ever.'

It was Holly who made the decision for her. She came to the door of the shop and stood there, a wan figure in school uniform. Her hair, washed free of its supportive gel, flopped silkily over her forehead and bristled like a worn, short-pile carpet around her neck and above her ears. She caught Cara's eye and she looked so miserable, so unsure beneath the defiant pout that Cara's heart went out to her. In mid-sentence, mid-argument, she took off her apron.

'All right. I'll come.'

Mario was philosophical about losing his assistant so soon. He approved of a man who came and took what he wanted. He embraced her once again and, as they left, plonked a carton in Mitch's arms.

'What is this?' demanded Mitch testily outside on the pavement.

'Bruised fruit,' she said.

'I'm sorry I asked.'

CHAPTER FIVE

THE evening newspaper being what it was, and the day being relatively un-newsworthy, the story about Holly's suspension was on page three.

'Page *three*!' Mitch moaned, throwing down the newspaper in disgust. He had finally arrived home at seven, by which time Cara had had several hours to settle in. She had packed at her flat and driven out in the Mini with Holly while Mitch obeyed the summons of Superwatch and his car telephone and raced back to his office.

'It's a lovely photo of Holly,' said Cara.

'Lovely? With that hair?'

'Oh—the hair, that's nothing. It'll be long again in no time. Her bone structure is great. Long hair concealed it.'

Mitch snorted. 'There's nothing to hide it now!' He went towards the stairs. 'If any reporter comes nosing around asking if we're going to fight the entire educational system over my daughter's right to wear her hair like a toothbrush, just——'

'I know. No comment,' she said brightly.

Cara had cooked a lamb casserole for dinner. Its fragrance filled the super kitchen as she sang and tossed a salad and piped cream on a chocolate soufflé. When she called Holly to provide the finishing touch the girl came eagerly to check the chocolate leaves she'd made. 'Wow!' she said, 'they turned out!' Tongue tucked in the corner of her mouth, she arranged them on the soufflé cream.

When Mitch came downstairs, showered and

changed into crisp leisure wear, he found the dining table set with casual elegance and Cara and Holly singing a top forty song together in the kitchen. He came to the servery and looked in rather nonplussed. Holly gave a shriek and shielded the soufflé from view.

'Go away, Dad, it's a surprise!' Which was such a change from mutinous sulks that he went away and fetched himself a drink, wandering back again and again as if intrigued by the goings on in the kitchen. When Holly finished her decorating, she whizzed upstairs and Mitch strolled in to watch Cara slice up some bread while she sang.

'You seem very happy, considering you didn't want to come,' he observed.

Cara shrugged. 'I prefer to be happy, so I am.'

'Is it that easy?' he queried sceptically, watching her relaxed movements as she tossed crusty bread chunks into a basket, then dropped a napkin over it.

'Not always.' She scraped off the breadboard and plucked up a corkscrew of cucumber peel from the floor. Leaning past him, she took aim and shot it across the room into the waste disposal sink. It draped itself half in, half out. 'I've had to work at it. Being happy can be really hard work,' she grinned.

Mitch leaned on a counter. 'Easier for people like you, though. Without commitment or responsibility, you only play games. You told me so yourself.'

'It was a joke, Mitch. I've had my share of pain and disappointments. But I choose to be happy anyway.'

'You just move on somewhere else—that's what you do. When things look like getting a bit tough, you pack up and run away and kid yourself that you're choosing to be happy.'

Cara picked up a carrot top, aimed it at the waste disposal and missed. 'What would you know about it,' she parried, aware that he had touched a weak spot. Hadn't she already considered moving on simply because she didn't want to get involved with him? So what on earth had possessed her to come here? Lord, she was crazy. Mitch went over and picked up the strewn scraps.

'I hope you don't play darts with the food we're eating,' he said.

Mitch seemed surprised that the meal was so good. Cara's casual way with food produced remarkable results. He ate everything, had second helpings and eyed her thoughtfully. He looked quite stunned by the chocolate soufflé.

'You made this?'

'And I made the chocolate leaves,' Holly told him. 'Cara showed me how.'

'Oh, did she?' murmured Mitch, and as Holly described the process, he appreciatively ate his soufflé and watched his animated daughter. 'Am I allowed to eat these works of art?' He indicated a chocolate leaf poised on his fork.

'Oh, sure. I can always make some more. Don't eat too much cream, Dad. You've got to watch your cholesterol level.'

He looked astounded. Cara choked a little on some dessert but turned innocent eyes to him. 'I suppose it's my own fault for insisting you come,' he muttered, but it was with amusement. 'Wonderful,' he told Cara as he helped himself to more dessert and a laughing Holly went to answer the phone. He glanced after his daughter. 'For all your haphazard ways, you have a sensitive touch.'

'Some people have green thumbs,' Cara said, waving away the compliment, 'I just have this affinity with food. Whatever I do to it, it likes me.'

'So I've noticed,' he said, savouring some soufflé

minus cream. 'But I wasn't talking about the food.'

The phone call was for him. It was the last they saw of him that night. He withdrew to his study and worked, poring over legal books and the information that gossiped through to him via his telex. He was up early and at breakfast took a phone call and made another at a lordly beep from Superwatch. Cara wondered how often he got up from meals to attend to some matter that counted more than his digestion. He winced less at Holly's hair that morning. Oddly enough, the tough punk haircut was just what was needed to point out that Holly's occasional tough smartness was all adolescent bravado.

Cleo called on Tuesday evening before Mitch arrived home. She smiled her rather charming smile, but Cara sensed a certain underlying hostility. Not unexpected. If a woman hoped to marry a man she wouldn't exactly be delighted when he drafted in someone else to live in his house.

Cleo bridled a bit when Cara offered her a drink. She went to the bar herself and fetched one, her movements swift and sure as if to emphasise her familiarity with this house.

'I wish Mitchell had asked me to stay with Holly. I could have taken some leave—he knows I'd do anything to help him and Holly.'

'Perhaps he didn't want to interfere with your work, and I am temporarily unemployed——' Cara suggested.

Cleo wandered about, touching this and that with wistful, possessive little flicks of her hands. 'He only had to ask. I'm a very close friend of the family,' she said, turning to Cara with one of those charming smiles. 'Very close.' The woman seemed to feel the need to explain just how close a friend she was. She had been at school with Holly's mother, she said.

'Goodness me, you couldn't get two more opposite girls—I was there on a scholarship, could hardly afford to buy my books—and Fran's father was a newly appointed judge and her mother a writer!' She laughed a little. 'But we became such good friends.' Best friend Fran had been clever, a sportswoman, a public speaker extraordinaire, Dux of the school. 'And I just struggled along—it was a bit like being the tail of a comet,' she smiled. Fran was attractive, popular, brilliant—honours and distinctions. Law studies.

'I was her bridesmaid.' Fran had made a spectacular bride. 'And I'm godmother to Holly.' She lapsed into silence for a while, and Cara felt the woman had almost forgotten anyone else was present. 'She always said she'd never have children. I was surprised when she said she was pregnant—children would drag her career down, she always said, and she was very ambitious.' She laughed again. 'Strange how things work out. I always said I wanted four children and here I am with none.'

Was that a trace of jealousy as well as affection for her tragic friend? Cara wondered. It would only be natural. In fact she might even have hated such a gifted, fortunate friend at times. She wondered about that phrase—'she always said she'd never have children'. Had Cleo ever said that in front of Holly? As an unimpeachable source, her godmother who loved her, if smotheringly and ineptly, would qualify. It might be enough to start the canker of doubt in a young, vulnerable adolescent, searching for identity and with memories of a brilliant, preoccupied mother.

Cara and Holly spent the days in companionship—swimming, sketching, experimenting with recipes. Mitch wasn't around much. He had struck a snag with the Japanese consortium's legal negotiations with the government, and his face grew tense and haggard. On Wednesday night it was nearly ten when he arrived home with the problem solved. He almost fell into a chair. Cara felt the strongest urge to go to him, smooth out the lines on his forehead, loosen his tie—lighten his load in some way. It had never been like this with Guy. Guy had always been carefree, a loving playmate. He'd never needed his brow smoothed, never needed to loosen up.

'Hard day, Mitch?' she asked.

'The worst,' he said, eyes shut.

Holly came in just then, eagerly holding aloft a kerosene lamp. 'I found it, I knew we had one somewhere—oh, Dad, you're home,' she said to her father who greeted her and stared at the lantern swinging from her hand. 'This is for our viewing party,' she explained. 'A Japanese viewing party. Well, it's hardly a party, because there's just Cara and me——'

Mitch looked to Cara for clarification. A Japanese viewing party, she told him, was a pleasant tradition intended to intensify one's observations by shutting off the distraction and noise of speech and allowing one's senses to tune to the sounds and the feel and the smell of the night. 'Meditation of a kind—we take a lantern and walk out single file somewhere in the garden, sit on the grass and turn out the light. Then we take a sip of plum wine—to sharpen our sense of taste—and sit a while not speaking, listening to the night and ourselves——'

Mitch let his head sink back on the chair, watched her through half-closed lids. 'And where did you come across this ritual? Japan?'

'Well, it was in Turkey, as a matter of fact, and I was travelling with a Swede and two Aussies and we met this Japanese couple——'

'All right, all right.' He held up his hands. 'Off you go. Not too much plum wine for Holly.'

Cara looked thoughtfully at his tense shoulders. She winked at Holly, picked up the bottle of plum wine and an extra glass. 'A good thing you're home, Mitch—three makes it a party.'

He opened his eyes again. 'Three? No, no—count me out, I'm tired.'

Cara took one of his arms. 'Come with us, Mitch.'

Holly took the other. 'Come on, Dad.'

He looked at them, his face oddly vulnerable for a moment. Then, with a wry smile, he allowed them to pull him up. 'All right, then. How long will this take?'

'Oh—maybe forty minutes.' Cara wondered for a moment if he was going to set Superwatch to keep them on schedule.

'This will be very interesting,' he said as he followed them out to the vine-covered patio. 'Forty minutes of silence from Cara Matheson? Surely an impossible dream?'

Holly giggled, and Cara shushed. 'No talking now, until we get back here.'

The lantern threw a jiggling, yellow oval ahead. They walked down the patio steps, their shoes clattered briefly on the stone pool surrounds, then Cara guided them across the inner-sprung lawns, skirted around the edge of whispering jungle garden down to an open patch of ground at the rear boundary. They sat down on the grass and Cara extinguished the light. The night was suddenly around them, black and thick, leavened gradually by starlight and moon as their eyes accepted the change. Cara took the stopper off the plum wine, went to Holly, poured a little in her upheld glass, moved on to Mitch. He looked up at her as she bent to serve him. Though only a few planes of his face, sheened by moonlight, were visible, his eyes

glittered, drawing hers and holding them for long
seconds. She poured the wine, heard it softly sigh into
his glass, then sat cross-legged to sip at her own wine
and look and listen and breathe the air.

The smell of grass and earth and the rich overlay of
Mr Welland's compost piles. Somewhere a faint,
elusive tang of mango wood and the sharpness of
eucalypts and lemon grass. Jasmine poured out its
perfume, floated it on the breeze that flirted this way
and that, cooling Cara's cheeks, lifting her hair. A
long way off an owl called, a lonely sound in the dark.
The creaking song of bamboo stems—the peacock's
single scream—the sea-swell rustle of gum leaves.
Cara looked up to a giddiness of stars. An indigo sky,
so beautiful, so immense. Tears sprang to her eyes at
its grandeur and she sat there—and sat—and knew
that Mitch was beside her and the universe was all
around her and never before had it been so right.

At length she lit the lamp again. Silently they
walked back over the grass and the slate to the house
and she extinguished the light.

Holly had tears streaming down her face. 'I looked
up and there was so much of it and I felt so——' she
said, half laughing, half crying. 'It's all there and I
never look—I never look——'

'You and me both, sweetheart,' said Mitch; he
hugged her close and over her head, looked at Cara.

Thursday. Cara woke very early and looked around
the room that was becoming familiar. Not yet three
days since she'd come here pretending that it was all
because of Holly. Fool! she told herself fiercely. You
wanted to come and look into his life—couldn't resist
it, and now look what you've done. But she leapt out of
bed, unwilling to put a name to what she'd done. Just a
kiss, that's all. So what? Don't answer that. She pulled
back the curtain and stuck her head out the window to

look at a new day of blue and gold. She breathed in deeply and had an overwhelming wish to be up high somewhere with the air crisp and still. And she knew just where.

Holly groaned when Cara woke her. 'Five-thirty?' she croaked disbelievingly.

'Why don't we drive up to the mountains today—do you like rainforests? A friend of mine works up near Beechmont—we might be able to go abseiling if we can borrow his ropes——'

Holly reached out and swivelled her digital clock closer. 'Five-*Thirty*?' she wailed, and pulled her bedclothes over her head. Cara waited. 'Rainforests?' a voice murmured a moment later. The bedclothes heaved and Holly's hedgehog hair appeared, then one eye. 'Abseiling?'

'You'll love it.' Cara laughed and went to the door. 'Jeans, shirt, trainers and a sweater. Gloves if you've got them—for abseiling.'

The girl was fully dressed when she came downstairs about half an hour later. Cara wore jeans and a sapphire blue tee-shirt, and her hair sprang in waves and curls from a rolled headband of blue and red. She had unearthed a vacuum flask and a large, round basket in which were already packed some fruit and slices of a cake made by Holly the day before. The girl tossed down gloves and sweater and started helping Cara with the sandwiches.

When Mitch appeared at the servery, it was to see Cara and his daughter both aim scraps of tomato at the disposal unit.

'Ready, set—*go*!' Cara called. Holly giggled. Both tomato end-pieces landed with little splots on the counter top.

'Oh, my God,' said Mitch, and they both swung around to him. He wore pyjama pants and a red dressing gown and his hair was quite extensively ruffled. His feet were bare. Cara hadn't seen him like this in the morning. Usually when he appeared for breakfast he looked as if he had passed along that assembly line—bzzzz, close shave—whhhst—spray of male cologne—swish, on with a crisp shirt, zip, up with the knife-creased trousers. A twist with the tie, a buff to the shoes and there he was, the perfect image of the professional man. Cara liked the pre-assembly model rather more.

Mitch stared at the sandwiches, the picnic basket. 'It's only six o'clock,' he said, and consulted his watch. Good lord, unshaven and barefooted but wearing Superwatch. Did he wear it everywhere—even to bed?

They explained about the trip to the mountains. 'I was going to check with you first, of course,' Cara said comfortably, 'It *is* all right, isn't it?'

'I—suppose so,' he said dubiously, and sat down to the breakfast table which was already set. Absently he fixed some cereal and ate as he watched Cara and Holly bustle about, listened as they talked about the trip. Made another double-miss at the disposal unit. Laughed.

He cleared his throat. 'I might take the day off and come too.'

Cara and Holly turned around as one. Stared at him.

'Take the day off?' said Holly in hushed tones. Mitch shifted in his seat.

'Yes, yes—take the day off. It's not a revolutionary idea—people do it all the time.'

'But *you* don't. You *never* take a day off—at least not since I was little——'

'Yes, well, I've just decided to, haven't I,' he said irritably. There was a faint flush of colour over his cheekbones. 'That is, if I'm welcome.'

Holly swallowed, bit her lip. Then she rolled her

eyes at Cara. 'Men are so *dense*!'

'Six more sandwiches?' Cara asked.

'Six more sandwiches.' Holly almost sang the words.

There was a spring in Mitch's step as he went to change.

'Jeans, shirt, trainers and sweater,' Holly called cheekily after him. 'And gloves for the abseiling.'

'Abseiling?' He came back, poked his head through the servery. 'No one mentioned abseiling.'

'I was going to check with you about that too, Mitch,' smiled Cara. 'I haven't got any ropes——'

'A disadvantage, surely.'

'—but I have a friend who lives at Beechmont——'

'—who *does* have ropes.'

'Uh-huh. If we can get some extra gear you can abseil too if you like. It's perfectly safe, I do assure you.'

'Oh, good,' he said meekly. 'As long as it's safe.'

By the time Mitch had made the numerous phone calls to release himself for the day, by the time he had pacified his phones and telex and facsimile machines, another hour was gone. They carried out their picnic supplies and Mitch headed off to the Peugeot's garage.

'Oh, no,' Cara told him. 'We're not going in your car.'

'Of course my car—what else?'

She pointed to her khaki Mini parked in readiness in the drive.

He laughed. 'You're kidding.' He sobered. 'You're not.'

'I'm not.' Cara went to her car, unlocked the boot.

'My car has more room, more power—we'll be more comfortable,' he pointed out, quite correctly.

'Your car also has a telephone, Mitch. If you imagine I'm going to drive towards the tranquillity of the mountains with your phone ringing, forget it. It's bad enough that you have to bring Superwatch along, but I suppose at least people can't send you messages on it,' she muttered as she set the basket in the boot.

'*Super*watch?' Mitch echoed. 'What the devil are you talking about?'

'That thing practically runs your life.'

Mitch glanced down at the gold watch. 'Nonsense.'

'It does—you don't even seem to know it, that's the worst of it—I mean, *why* are you wearing it now? It's a day off.'

'Why am I wearing it?' He stared at her, mystified, then shook his head. He looked down into the boot, caught sight of the old bowler hat crammed into a corner and pounced on it.

'Why are you carrying *this* around with you?' He knocked out the dents in the crown with his knuckles. 'A moth-eaten busker's bowler hat! And you've got the nerve to ask me why I'm wearing a watch!'

'It has sentimental value.' She snatched it from him. 'I always keep it with me——'

Mitch snorted. 'Okay. I'll accept that you carry a bowler around with you because you're fond of it if you'll accept that I wear a watch for all the usual reasons.' Cara thrust the hat into the boot again, feeling just a bit foolish.

'We go in my car,' she insisted mulishly.

He gave in and they piled into the Mini, stopping off at Cara's place to fetch her abseil gear. 'I'll just be a minute,' she said, but they went in with her, following close behind. 'Anyone would think I was the Pied Piper,' she said lightly as she unlocked the door.

'Aren't you?' said Mitch.

Cara tiptoed in, frowned at Pete who was asleep, slumped over the table. Then she went through to collect her climbing harnesses and helmets. The clink of metal woke Pete who sat up, unbothered by the presence of Mitch and Holly at such an hour. He got up, grinning, and picked Cara up, whirling her around, harness flying.

'I did it!' he said, jubilant.

'Pete, put me down. Did what?'

'It. *It*. Posted it yesterday.'

'Fantastic!' She wrapped her arms around his neck and kissed his cheek. 'Congratulations!'

Pete had just proposed to Vivian, she explained to Holly and Mitch. 'A feat of enormous courage.'

Danny emerged from his bedroom, surveyed the visitors and gave one of his early morning grunts that sufficed as 'hello'.

'Can we borrow a guitar, Danny? An old acoustic?' Cara asked, feeling rather self-conscious about this family trio of which she was part. 'We', she had said. Danny obligingly took one off the wall.

'Will you be able to drag yourself away to play with me as usual tomorrow night?' he asked, with a curious look at Mitch and the abseil gear.

'Of course. Even housekeepers get time off,' she joked, then to Pete, 'we'll celebrate when Viv writes back to say yes.'

They were just about to drive away when Pete came flying out, an anguished look on his face.

'I just thought of something,' he said. 'What if she says no?'

CHAPTER SIX

THE mountain air was chill. Clean. And deep in the rainforest where the sun filtered down through a canopy of ash and cedar and fig, the air was green. A delicate haze around mighty, fluted trunks, around lacework figs with their flying buttresses—around colonnades of tree-ferns, giant leaves overlapped into perfect Gothic arches. In the cathedral quiet, leaves dropped on their long see-saw journey down from sunlight to land with sharp, small cracks on rocks or the forest floor. The air was rich with the smell of moist decay, the rotting wood of forest giants long dead yet host for mosses smooth and shaggy, for tiny architectural eaves of white fungi with grooved orange undersides and orchids and the shining, crinkled fronds of crows' nests. The smell of life and death and life renewed. The only sounds—falling leaves, the twit-twit of birds up high, the ceremonial call of the whip-bird—were so right that they seemed not to be sounds at all, simply a variation on silence.

Softly they trod on the track, listening for the sounds of silence, not speaking. Voices and words did not belong in here where the world was the way it used to be before voices and words changed everything. The breeze stirred the canopy. Hush. A flit of wings. A falling leaf.

Beep, beep, beep, beep! Cara whirled around. Mitch stared at her, startled, disorientated, then snapped off the wristwatch alarm. 'I forgot it was still set——' he muttered. Cara glared at the watch She was beginning to hate it as if it had a personality. A

demanding, possessive personality that never quite let
him free of his work even here where a falling leaf was
an event.

'Couldn't you have left that thing in the car?' she
said crossly.

Mitch looked at her levelly. 'With your bowler hat?'

Cara turned away and led off again. 'At least my
bowler doesn't beep,' she muttered, then hoped they
hadn't heard. It sounded utterly idiotic.

They took the border track turn off to Tullawallal,
came to a rocky outcrop and ancient stands of
Antarctic beech trees. The stubs of old trunks still
remained, splotched with lichens, cushioned and
veloured in mosses. The 'new' trunks, mere hundreds
of years old, soared upwards. Millions of beautiful red-
brown leaves lay on the forest floor. The trees were
reminders of an earlier, cooler, wetter climate and
were dying here in their most northward location on
the continent. Now their seeds no longer grew. When
these trunks died, it would be the end of a long struggle
to adapt.

'How old are they?' asked Holly, clambering around
the dead and living trunks with her camera.

'Maybe two thousand years old. The first of these
might have been growing here while Christ was
turning water into wine on the other side of the world
. . . miracles . . .' Cara said. She touched the venerable
wood and dreamed a little. And Mitch and Holly
dreamed with her.

They ate their picnic lunch in the open near the
Lamington National Park's entrance—shared it with
glossy black and white currawongs and two aggressive
male brush turkeys with scrawny red heads and
collapsed yellow balloon necks. Holly fetched Danny's
guitar at Cara's prompting and strummed softly at
some basic chords.

Mitch frowned. 'Where did you learn to play?'

'At school. I borrow my friend's guitar at lunchtime and she shows me some new chords——' A little later she stopped playing when a girl and boy about fourteen and sixteen emerged from the nearby camping area and stood watching.

'Can you play an A minor progression?' the boy asked.

Holly shook her head. 'What's that?'

Cara lazed in the sun, her eyes closed, lips curved in a smile as the boy showed Holly the chord progression and said what a pity she was only here for the day because they had a campfire party going that night and he needed someone to play rhythm while he played melody. With Mitch's permission Holly went off with her new friends and little while later there came on the still air, the sounds of two guitars and a young, sweet voice. Cara's smile grew.

'All right, all right—so I shouldn't have pushed her into taking flute lessons——' said Mitch, close by, 'I should have let her learn the guitar as she wanted.'

She grinned, opened one eye. 'I didn't say a word.'

'You just may be more dangerous when you say nothing.'

She turned her head. He was stretched out beside her on the grass, hands clasped under his head as he squinted up at a fathomless blue sky across which little white clouds scooted.

'I'm not dangerous at all,' she protested mildly, closing her eyes again. This too was perfect, she thought—just as sitting in the dark last night had been complete, so now was this contentment with the sun warming her through the crisp, clean air and the sound of Holly's laughter coming with her music through the trees, and Mitch right here beside her.

'The most dangerous woman I know.'

'Why?' she asked huskily, when she knew she ought to make some quip, some smart comment to break up this languorous, beguiling mood.

'Because you make me forget what I always remember——' She opened her eyes. He was leaning over her—Mitch, against a blue, blue sky. '—and you make me remember what I thought I'd forgotten.'

One of the brush turkeys came to peck and rustle in the lunch wrappings and a circus of currawongs swooped and dived for their share of the crumbs. Cara saw nothing but Mitch looking down at her. He bent and kissed her—simply, sweetly—rubbing his lips across hers with tenderness. Affection. She lifted her arms about his neck and he rolled closer, touching her face and her tangled, spread hair with drifting, small movements of his hands. It wasn't sexual at all—no drumbeats in her ears, no heat save that of the sun, no boiling, roiling desire. It went with the peace of the place, the unhurried pace of the forest and the mountains where a hundred years was no more than a day and a night.

'Steady on there, me old darlings—this is a family place, you know.'

Cara and Mitch broke apart—looked up. A red-headed man stood there watching them, his weight thrown on to one leg, hand on hip and a great kookaburra grin on his freckled face. In fact, the resemblance to that bird was marked. His eyes were small and bright and alert and he regarded Cara and Mitch with head tilted to one side. His nose thrust out beakily and his hair thrust up like feathers. For all that he was immensely attractive. 'A bit of splendour in the grass?' he asked, grinning and waggling his eyebrows.

'Steve!' Cara leapt up. The man held his arms out and she dived into them, hugging him.

'Recognised the hair,' Steve explained, touching the

abundant, tangled mass. 'Hasn't it been declared a national wilderness yet?' He directed a friendly, speculative look at Mitch and Cara disengaged herself to introduce the two men.

Steve Roswell shared a house with several others further down the mountain and worked as general climbing and walking guide, social organiser and sometime bartender at the lodge just a few minutes from here. On their way up, they had left a message for him at his house. Mitch shook hands with him, his smile a bit stiff, his eyes dropping to take in the firm grip Steve had around Cara's waist.

'Brought the ropes and the extra set of climbing gear you asked for—over there.' Steve indicated a Range Rover parked nearby. 'I've got an hour to spare,' he grinned. 'Want me to come along and check that you haven't forgotten your knots?'

'Yes, please,' she said promptly.

'Very flattering,' Steve laughed.

'You're a good man to have on a rope.'

'To have on a rope?' he repeated, opening his eyes wide. 'Sounds kinky, darling, that could be misunderstood. You'll shock Mitch!'

Mitch snorted. 'Not possible.'

Steve laughed, clasped his arm tighter around her and looked down into her eyes, suddenly serious. 'I was real sorry to hear about Guy. Must have been rough on you.'

'At the time I thought I'd die too,' she said simply, then, conscious of Mitch's arrested attention, 'shall we go?'

They drove, the Mini behind Steve's 4WD, past the camping site and tooted the horn for Holly, who came out carrying Danny's guitar. Reluctantly she waved goodbye to her friends.

At the beginner's cliff, Steve performed what Cara

supposed was his standard 'pep' talk given to lodge
guests who tackled abseiling for the first time. It was a
masterly blend of firm warnings, comedy and reassurance. Holly listened, giggled a lot and sobered as she
followed instructions on gearing up. As Steve and
Cara set up the safety and climbing ropes, utilising
several trees scarred from years of similar service,
Mitch helped his daughter and donned his own gear.

'You catch on fast,' said Cara as she checked his
tape knots. Mitch looked at her solemnly from under
his helmet.

'I try,' he replied. Cara squinted at him suspiciously
as she went over the cliff edge to demonstrate, while
Steve explained each move to a very nervous Holly. As
she lowered herself out of sight of the others, she saw
Mitch bend and say something to his daughter—
something that made her look up at him in surprise.

Cara spread her feet and pushed and bounced off
the cliff face, paying out her rope bit by bit, relaxing as
the rhythm came back to her. She swung in under a
shelf and lowered her feet to the ground, shouted
'Down' and released her ropes which slithered
upwards immediately.

Holly came next, slowly at first, rhythmically as she
began to trust the ropes and her own control. She
tumbled to the ground and Cara steadied her.

'I don't know if I love it or hate it,' she panted, face
alight with achievement, 'but I want to do it again—
can I?'

'Sure.'

Holly waited to see her father's descent—a very
smooth affair, very controlled, very confident. Not a
first descent.

'He really can!' Holly exclaimed. 'I never knew—he
told me just now he's done it before——'

'Did he really?' Cara put her hands on her hips and

thought of her patronising remarks to him as a rank beginner.

'He said he was so scared the first time that he almost backed out——' Holly waved an arm as her father swung free below the rock overhang. 'Terrific, Dad—I'm going up for another go——' She was gone, haring up the rocky track worn by multitudes of beginners. Mitch looked down at Cara.

'Are you sure this is perfectly safe?' he mocked.

'Very funny. How often have you done this?'

He slid down the remainder of the drop using the rope only, and landed on his feet. 'I used to come up here on summer camp as a kid,' he said as he released his ropes. 'I did my first abseil on this cliff.' He shouted to Steve and the ropes snaked upwards. 'In my Uni days I belonged to a bushwalking club——' He breathed in deeply and looked around at the valley spread out way below the ledge on which they stood, at the mountains hazed with the blue-purple of afternoon, at the tiny plateau lime-green in the sunshine, its miniature farmhouse silver-roofed, its road a pencilled-in S. 'I'd forgotten how good it was——' His eyes came back to hers—a boy's eyes, enthusiastic and glowing. Was this one of the things she'd made him remember? Cara began up the track.

'I wish you'd told me you weren't a tyro climber,' she said crossly.

'You jumped to conclusions so beautifully,' he called after her. 'It was a consolation to see someone else do it as thoroughly as I did myself.'

But he might have jumped to a few more during the afternoon, Cara thought later when Steve had taken his ropes and gear and departed with a cheery wave. Her friendship with Steve went back a long way— before Guy. They had met in Wales and, in the peculiar way of backpackers staying at youth hostels,

ran into each other again in Italy where they'd
climbed together. He had a free and easy way about
him, did Steve; he was lovable and affectionate and
they shared similar views, and she wasn't quite sure
just why she'd never responded to his considerable
efforts to take her to bed. He'd accepted it philosophi-
cally and made a friend of her instead. Friends they
had remained, exchanging occasional postcards,
sending messages through mutual touring friends.
This was the first time she'd actually seen him since
Guy's death. But Mitch might have misinterpreted
their familiarity and Steve's occasional wicked
squeeze of her rump. He was rather quiet as the Mini
chugged reluctantly back up the mountain; he was
absorbed in some inner thoughts as they took a final
stroll into the rainforest. When they emerged, Mitch
picked up his pace, looked at his watch and Cara saw
that for him the day was over.

'Expecting a phone call tonight, Mitch?' she asked,
and he nodded.

'A very important call from the States. Eight-thirty.'

'Relax,' she soothed. 'We'll be back with hours to
spare.'

But they weren't.

At eight-thirty they were still on the mountain with
a Mini that had chugged its last coming up from the
abseil cliff—with the nearest mechanic out somewhere on a tractor job and the next nearest mechanic
out of spare parts for Minis.

At eight-thirty, Mitch was grim-faced, having
passed through every possible phase. Disbelief: 'It
must start—let *me* try.' Firm Male Optimism: 'We
should have it fixed in an hour——' The Search for
Alternatives: 'If we can't get it fixed we'll take a bus
back.' Irritation: 'But there *must* be another bus!'
Explosiveness: 'Stay here tonight? *Stay*? Are you

mad? I'm expecting an important phone call——' Icy Resignation: 'Very well. I'll book rooms at the Lodge.'

More Disbelief: 'No rooms? None at all?' Sarcasm: 'Yes, I've no doubt your friend Steve would give *you* a bed for the night—but *three* of us?' Extreme Sarcasm: 'But of course—he's got a full house with two Canadian birdwatchers and a German astronomer. Typical of your friends——'

Ridicule: 'Borrow a tent—a *tent*? If you think I'm going to spend the night up here on a mountain, crouched in a *tent* with two females——'

At eight-thirty Mitch was hammering a tent-peg into the ground. He looped a rope around it and glared over at Cara who was doing likewise on the other side of the tiny two-man canvas that would just, only just, squeeze in the three of them.

'This wouldn't have happened if I'd brought *my* car,' he glowered.

'It might,' Cara retorted defensively. She was dying to laugh but dared not. Though she was dismayed by the turn of events, initially stricken by the prospect of repair costs, she had whizzed through each phase quicker than Mitch, used as she was to adapting to the unexpected and the uncomfortable. Now, even with the obvious problems of sharing a tent to come, she could see the humour of it. Out of his *métier*, his comforts unforthcoming, his beard beginning to show, his clothes grubby from grappling first with the car and now with the camping gear borrowed from a highly amused Steve, Mitch was like a scowling boy.

Their borrowed sleeping bags were laid out inside the tent; their borrowed lantern hung from a low tree branch. With borrowed towels they went to the showers. Cara was back first, her skin glowing, her soul at peace in the beauty of the mountain night. She spread one of their picnic rugs outside the tent, then

set out a jointed cold chicken, donated by a friend of
Steve's—uncorked a bottle of white wine and poured
some into wineglasses—these last donated by Steve
himself. Holly, quite unashamedly delighted at the
disaster, had been at the campfire party since seven
with her new friends and by the sound of it, with most
of the other campers. Through the trees Cara could see
the glow of the fire and hear the mellow strum of
guitars. When Mitch stomped back, his towel slung
around his neck, Cara was sitting cross-legged on the
rug softly playing her flute.

His steps slowed as he came into the light, and his
eyes played over the spread rug, the food, the wine.
And Cara playing the pure, lingering notes of 'The
Shepherd's Song.' When she finished she sat there,
looking up at him. Suddenly he laughed—threw back
his head.

'My God—what more could a man want? Shelter——' he waved a hand at the tent, 'food and wine
and a lovely woman making music——' his voice
trailed off huskily and he sat down facing Cara. 'And
here I was thinking I was in the wilderness.'

They ate and propped themselves against the tree,
one each side of it, sipping their wine.

'I haven't done this for years——' Mitch sighed,
head tipped up to the sky.

'Why haven't you?'

'Work—there never seems to be time——' He
lapsed into silence and Cara said nothing, but waited.
'I always planned to do what you've done—I wanted
to defer my final year at Uni, take two pairs of jeans, a
sweater and some tee-shirts and hike around
Europe——'

Over by the campfire, voices joined, singing 'Mull
of Kintyre'. Far off, a mopoke called across the ridges
and valleys.

'When you told me about Greece that night it reminded me—a year I was going to have, roaming the Greek countryside, Italy, France's vineyards. I'd planned to go with some friends.'

'What happened?'

'Oh—my father had a heart attack and it was touch and go for a time, so I stayed and studied instead because it became more urgent that I qualify and get involved with the practice—and then I met Fran and we married in our final year ... Holly came along sooner than we planned, and suddenly we weren't just students but parents——' He gave a huff of laughter, talked a bit about Holly's babyhood, the mistakes and the pleasures of parenting, and there was nothing in it to confirm Holly's fears that she wasn't wanted. Without strain Mitch spoke of Fran, and an image formed of a brilliant young woman who loved her family even if her career did take most of her time. 'We always wanted more children, but—it didn't happen, not until we'd given up on the idea, anyway——'

Cara gazed up at the sky, conscious of a tiny unworthy prickle of envy for poor Fran whom Mitch had loved. 'Was your wife happy about the new baby?'

'She was excited—the doctors warned her there might be complications, but she didn't want to believe that. She kept buying baby things in secret—couldn't resist it. She felt sheepish about it——'

Mitch talked on desultorily, skipping back and forth in time, and she began to see how his life had shaped up. His commitments and responsibilities had simply overtaken him before he'd ever had the chance to take his two pairs of jeans and go hiking. Though he didn't say so outright, she gathered that he had assumed other family responsibilities to spare his father's health, had inherited places on boards like

Carrington's, and committees for the same reason. Perhaps it was inevitable that his life was governed by machines and Superwatch. It had got out of hand though, she thought. Way out of hand. Mitch smiled over a boyhood recollection, picked up the wine bottle and leaned over to fill her glass. 'You see what I mean,' he said softly, 'you make me remember——'

'Is that good or bad?'

'Good. I've spent the last three years trying so hard to protect myself from memories that hurt that I've neglected all the good ones——' He was still for a moment, his face close to hers as he leaned around the tree trunk. It was perfectly natural that he should kiss her. Lightly—a sweet, affectionate encore to those earlier kisses in sunlight. Then again—less sweet, more sensual, his mouth open over hers, his tongue slipping between her lips, to taste the wine and be tasted. There was no other point of contact, just their lips yet every nerve in Cara's body was touched, twanging with sensation as the pressure of his kiss deepened and her head tilted back against the tree's rough bark. He drew away, breathing roughly, eyes half closed. Cara gave a foolish laugh. Mitchell Robert James Kirby had the shadow of a beard, his hair was roughed up, his eyes warm, his mouth—that mouth she had once thought was set in concrete—parted still from kissing her. She lifted a hand and stroked one finger down his roughened jaw.

'This is a funny place for us to be.'

'It wouldn't have happened if I'd brought *my* car.' But this time it sounded entirely different.

Later she played the flute again and he lay stretched out, watching her. When she stopped he said, 'Tell me about Guy.'

But she played once more before she told him.

'I met him in Paris. He was an American there to

study violin. We fell in love. Moved in together——'
she smiled faintly. 'Our room overlooked a bakery.
Everything always smelled of fresh bread . . .' She
looked up at the sky. 'It was wonderful, and then one
day after breakfast he went out with his violin and—
never came back. He was hit by a car.'

The lantern flickered as it ran out of fuel. Mitch got
up to turn it off and the night rushed in, no longer held
off by the pale light. He sat down beside her on the
rug. Cara felt his warmth.

'If Guy had lived, would you have married him—
had children?'

'We never talked about for ever——'

'You never wanted more—to settle down?'

'No,' she said firmly. 'I never did.'

'Then maybe Guy wasn't the right man——'

Cara jerked away from him. 'Oh—you don't think
so? Guy was *exactly* right for me. He knew how to live,
how to laugh—he knew the important things in life—
he took the time to smell the flowers.'

'But you didn't talk about for ever.'

'Heavens, Mitch—do you think a relationship can
only resolve itself in—wedding rings and—a cosy little
house somewhere with a picket fence and babies
and——'

'Don't you want babies?'

'No. Yes! I mean—not if it means falling into a
trap. Before you know it the wedding rings are
tarnished and the cosy little house is too small to keep
you from each other's throats and the babies just get in
the way—just excess baggage—and what started as
love ends up twisted into resentment and hate——'

'A trap, Cara? Is that what it was for your parents?'

Once again he had homed in on the key word. Cara
made a conscious effort to calm herself. How had she
allowed this emotional subject loose?

'Oh dear—I keep forgetting I'm talking to a lawyer. All these shrewd questions; you'd be dynamite in cross-examination. Have you ever considered going to the bar, Mitch?' she said lightly, and to her relief he went along with the change of subject.

'To tell the truth, I don't think I could make it as a barrister,' he said solemnly.

'Why not? All that rhetoric would suit you. Why, in your office that day you actually said, "Be that as it may"!'

'Really? Well, be that as it may, I probably won't go to the bar. It's the wig.'

'The wig?' She queried.

'I look like Captain Cook in the wig.'

She giggled. 'Or a Regency rake. Or Prince Charming——' It seemed so long ago—the night she'd lost her shoe and fallen in the garden with him. She should have run away like Cinderella.

'I nearly kissed you that night,' he murmured, keying accurately into her thoughts.

'But your watch sounded the alarm and brought you to your senses.'

He touched her shoulder and she turned instantly to him, her heart booming away like a kettle drum. Mitch pulled her backwards so that she was lying across his knees, and as he bent over her, touching his mouth to her throat, she wound her arms around his neck. When his lips found hers, she kissed him passionately, arching her body as his hands swept over her thighs, her breasts, then slipped beneath her sweater. Cara snatched at her control, spread her hands to his head, pushed him upwards away from her.

'Will your watch sound the alarm tonight, Mitch?' she asked, breathlessly. He looked down at her and his breathing slowed.

'I'll do better than that,' he said drily, standing up. 'Why don't you turn in, Cara? I'll go and bring Holly home.'

She crawled inside the tent, took off all but her tee-shirt and briefs and slipped into a sleeping bag. Wide-eyed, she lay in the dark. The happiness that had marked her day was dulled. It always happened when she thought of home and the parents who remained together enjoying fleeting moments of amity among the misery they'd made out of love. So absorbed had they always been in themselves and their love/war that she and her brother Simon had been mere incidentals. At twenty-nine, Simon had just survived his second divorce—both his marriages were casualties of his childhood, Cara believed. He wasn't able to make the conventional business of marriage, home and children work. As for her, she wasn't sure she even wanted to try.

Mitch was gone a long time. She strained to hear his voice and Holly's, tensed when he pulled aside the tent flap and entered in silence.

'Holly?' she said. Mitch brushed past her as he lowered himself to a sleeping bag.

'She's already asleep. Her friend's mother tucked her up in a spare sleeping bag in their tent. We're invited over for breakfast.'

'Oh, that's nice,' she said inanely. The tiny tent shrank suddenly. Cara became aware of every movement he made. The shush as he pulled off his sweater. Two soft thuds—shoes. The clink of a belt buckle, the short brrrt of his trousers zip and the rustle of denim as he discarded his jeans. She closed her eyes tight, but the visual images formed to match the sounds. Mitch in briefs, his long legs muscular and hairy—his shirt waiting to be unbuttoned. She clenched her hands as she imagined herself lying over him, unfastening the buttons, bending to put her mouth to his chest, running her fingertips over his ribs and his stomach and . . . desire rushed through her, a surge of power that heated her, damped her skin, brought a fierce, wanting ache. All she had to do was reach out. Cara lay stiffly, resisting the urge. Resisting the vibrations emanating from Mitch. One move was all it would take, she knew. Just one. And she was tempted, so tempted. Her physical need became a torment. She was only human, she rationalised desperately—other women fulfilled their needs without making such an issue of it. She could make love with Mitch and then just—just what? Make love with Mitch and you'll start thinking about for ever, because that's the kind of man he is.

She forced a yawn. Quite artistic, it was. The yawn of a woman tired out after an active day—a woman immune to the vibrant sexual messages in the air with nothing on her mind but sleep.

' 'night, Mitch,' she mumbled, and his reply came curtly.

'Good night.'

It was dawn when she woke, the remnant of some dream leaving a smile on her lips. She felt deliciously safe and warm, her arm hooked around a pillow the way she always slept. Except this pillow was large and warm. She moved her hand a little, eyes drowsing. Her fingertips found a marvellous, smooth texture, a beautiful, satisfying curve. She sighed, smiled wider, let her hand drift over and up until her fingers pushed into thick, springy hair. Cara's eyes opened. Mitch was close beside her, a bare arm and shoulder protruding from his unzipped sleeping bag. His arm curved about her waist—her hand was in his hair.

'Hello——' he murmured, green eyes heavy with sleep.

'Hello,' she smiled, and stretched a little, not taking her hand from his hair—no, that seemed right. A perfect way to wake. Mitch raised himself on one elbow.

'I've been dreaming about you,' he told her, and kissed her mouth. Last night's desire flared again—a fire that had not burnt out but had smouldered—and she kissed him back wildly, clenching her hand in his hair to urge him closer. She freed her other arm and held him, running her hands feverishly over his back, down to the taut muscles of his hips. He groaned, found the zipper of her part-unfastened sleeping bag, slid it slowly down, watching the sides fall apart. Her tee-shirt had rolled up to her breasts, her bikini pants had slipped a little. With a deep exhalation of breath, he laid his open palm across her abdomen. His thumb dipped into her navel, and she tensed as he bent and kissed the bare skin, delicately traced the tiny hollow with tongue tip while his hands—ah, his hands thrust up beneath the tee-shirt to knead the soft flesh and tease her nipples between finger and thumb.

'I've been dreaming of this——' Mitch growled, and pushed aside the tee-shirt to cradle a breast in both hands. Then he tenderly suckled until Cara arched against him in pleasure and he cradled her other breast and began the beguilement all over again.

Her hands slipped down beneath the skimpy briefs and spread over his bare buttocks. His body tensed, clenched. Mitch dragged in a huge breath and raised his head. They stared at each other, amazed at the distance they had travelled. Daylight brightened the tent. Birds twit-twitted in the trees. Voices reached them from a distance. Nearer.

Hastily they broke apart. Mitch crouched and dragged on his jeans. Cara pulled down her tee-shirt and stuck her legs back in the sleeping bag as Holly whipped aside the tent flap.

'Hey, breakfast, you two.' Her hair was standing on
end and her clothes were a mess, but she glowed. Too
late to don his shirt, Mitch held it like a shield in front
of his jeans zipper. He ruffled his daughter's hair. 'Hi,'
he said. 'It must be mountain madness, but I think I'm
even getting to like your hair!'

Holly grinned, looked from him to Cara with a
fleeting speculation. 'Hurry up—bacon and eggs
under the gum trees. Yum!' She sniffed the smell of
bacon and wood-smoke and took off. Mitch went to
the showers.

Mountain madness, Cara thought as she dressed.
Now *that* would be a nice, harmless affliction. You
could always drive down off a mountain and leave the
madness behind.

CHAPTER SEVEN

FRIDAY. Cara played with Danny as usual. The Mall was ablaze and a-bustle. Mrs Franklin went by with a balding man, presumably Mr Franklin and Danny broke into 'The Tennessee Waltz'. The woman was so delighted at being remembered that she came over and dropped a shower of coins in the bowler hat. Later two women stopped to listen to their music. Mother and daughter, Cara thought. The girl wore sunglasses and tilted her head to listen.

'A friend of yours?' murmured Cara to Danny as the girl, guided by her mother, came over. Rhonda, her name was. Hardly the 'kid' he said he'd been teaching. She was about twenty with long, fair hair and a mouth at once wilful and vulnerable. It was apparent that a few bridges had been crossed since she'd thrown her guitar at Danny.

'Are you coming home tonight?' Danny asked later. 'I'm tired of watering your petunias.'

'Keep them alive a bit longer for me. Mitch has to work late tonight. Holly's shopping with her friends, so I'll take her home and stay.'

Danny gave a wry smile. 'Sounds to me like you might stay for ever!'

For ever, Cara thought as she sat with Holly later still, teaching her to knit while a part of her strained to hear Mitch's arrival home. When his car purred along the drive and she knew he was near, it was as if a small part of her sprang to life. When he came in, his face drawn, his hand rubbing at his stomach she felt the sharp pang of concern. I'll bet he hasn't eaten since

breakfast, she thought. Someone should tell him he'll
wreck his health if he keeps this up. Someone should
make sure he eats properly—someone. Mitch looked
across at them—Holly at Cara's feet, her spiky head
bent over some red knitting, Cara leaning forward,
her hand outstretched to guide the wool, and behind
them the big room, elegant yet intimate with the
chairs drawn up close together and lamplight spilling
over. Holly displayed her knitting.

'Cara showed me how—when I get better at it, I
might knit you a sweater,' she said, and Mitch gravely
inspected the gappy, irregular purl and plain and said
with commendable tact and sincerity that he would
love her to knit him a sweater. His eyes met Cara's
over his daughter's head, and as he smiled, the tired
lines on his face diminished and she felt a great wash
of contentment that she had somehow helped it to
happen. She smiled too but turned away, shaken by
the gentle power of the homey little scene.

Later she was shaken again by another kind of
power. It was after one in the morning and, sleepless,
she rose at last, pulled on a dressing gown to cover her
nakedness and let herself out on to the upstairs
veranda. There was a light breeze blowing and a drift
of cloud across a moody moon. She stood for a while,
her skin cooling, tingling, until she sensed she was not
alone. She whirled around, her back to the balustrade,
hands gripping it either side of her.

Mitch stood there, bare-chested, wearing only short
pyjama pants. The moon emerged from cloud as he
came close to her, not speaking. Cara tried to think of
something to say—something prosaic and mood-
killing, for the atmosphere was spiced with danger.
But though her mouth opened, no words would come,
and the silence added a new dimension. Close he
came, so close that his bare legs brushed against hers.

Her mouth opened again and he bent and covered it with his, licking at her lips and inside them with slow, lazy strokes; Cara held on to the railing with both hands and wondered if the sleeplessness and the moody moon and this were all a dream. Mitch touched her waist and her pulses thundered in undreamlike urgency. His hands closed around her breasts and she gasped, grabbed protestingly at his arms. Gently he disengaged, took her wrists and returned her hands to the railing. Then with exquisite delicacy he un-wrapped her dressing gown, holding it aside to look at her. With a deep, indrawn breath he let one side of the jacket drop, ran fingertips over her ribs, her breast. So light was his touch that Cara could not distinguish between the breeze's caress and his. Her head dropped back and she sighed up at the moon that sulked beneath a cloud. Mitch's touch firmed. He held her breasts, lifted them and fondled, and her sigh turned to gasps of pleasure. She looked down, trembling with excitement to watch his hands on her—long fingers curved around pale flesh, thumbs rubbing, teasing.

'Ah——' she breathed, and her hands slipped down his arms, all the way down from his beautiful, smooth biceps to hair-spattered forearms to his wrists. And then her hands covered his on her breasts and she felt her own heartbeat pounding against her palm. She stilled. Mitch looked a question at her, his eyes glittering. For long moments she fought her silent battle, licked her lips and finally shook her head. She ducked away from him, dragged the dressing gown close around her and flew back to her bedroom. And to sleeplessness and the glow and fade of moody moonlight.

In the morning she packed her bag and brightly announced that she was leaving. She pointed out to a disappointed Holly that her grandparents would be

back from New York and no doubt pleased to have
her to stay next week—and as this was a weekend, she
herself wasn't needed. Holly went off in a sulk.

'She'll recover,' Cara told Mitch. 'Goodbye, then.
I've already put my bag in the Mini. I suppose I'll see
you in the Mall next Friday night——'

'Next Friday night—as if nothing's changed?' he
growled. 'What about us, Cara?'

'Us? There is no *us*, Mitch.'

'There's something between us, Cara. You're not
going to be a complete coward and deny that, are you?'

'*Something*, Mitch?' she said scathingly. 'Do you
want to put a name to it? Physical attraction? Lust?'

He came for her and she retreated until she wound
up against the dishwasher and he caught her by the
shoulders. 'Lust?' he repeated savagely. 'Is that the
only label you can come up with? Dammit, Cara, I
can't wait to get home to find you here—yesterday
when I woke and found you next to me I thought—yes,
this is right. This is the way I want to wake up every
day——' He shook her. 'I see you with my daughter
and I get this feeling . . . I don't know . . .' he stopped
and gave her another inarticulate little shake. 'I can't
even look at the damned *sky* without thinking about
you! I hadn't even bothered to look up until you came.'
He pulled her upwards suddenly, wrapping his arms
around her as if to bind her to him, and he kissed her
angrily as if it was all her fault that he thought about
her. Glowering, he dragged his mouth from hers,
stared into her face. 'I love you, dammit!' he accused.
His eyes widened as the words sank in. Mouth
working, he touched her hair, stroked its wild, springy
masses and everything he'd said, every move he'd
made touched a chord in Cara.

'I love you,' he whispered, cradling her close. Cara
leaned her head on his shoulder, clasped her arms

about his waist. I only wanted to make him smile, that was all, she thought. And now look. The words would not be denied. 'I love you, Mitch,' she said. He let out a great sigh, rested his cheek against her hair and for long moments they stood there, swaying back and forth a little in each other's arms, lost in dreams. Cara tensed, pulled back a little.

'This is crazy,' she said. 'It can't work.'

'We *are* different, but——'

'There's no future in it, Mitch—that's why I didn't want to get involved. I don't want your kind of life——'

He seized on it. 'But you've liked it these last few days. You liked being with me, with Holly. You made us a family again.'

'That's temporary, Mitch. And I told you, I make it a habit to be happy and I always am, just as long as I'm free to go when I want to——'

'Run away, you mean,' he said harshly, releasing her. 'All this moving on for fun and freedom is cowardice, Cara. You don't have to make your parents' mistakes. You're twenty-five. Why don't you stick around this time and see what happens?'

She ran her tongue over her lips—thought of that slip of paper pinned on her notice board. Names and addresses of future friends. She could pack up and leave for Cairns this week.

'Why don't we at least try?' he urged softly, keeping his distance, watching her across the kitchen. 'This has happened so fast. Why don't we take it easy—see each other—find out if we can make it work?'

Cara shook her head. 'It won't——' She moved towards the doorway, but he caught her wrist, held her.

'All right, Cara. Tell me you never want to see me again and I'll stop trying.' He hauled her in. 'Tell me,' he commanded, and wound his arms around her, nuzzled into her neck. 'Tell me, Cara, that you don't want me in your life.' He pressed kisses to her temple, her ear, her neck. 'Don't want me to hold you.'

'Mitch——' she gasped, as he fondled her hips.

'Just tell me——' he breathed, curving a hand to her breast, rubbing a thumb over the nipple raised and thrusting beneath her tee-shirt, '—and I'll give up.'

'Mitch,' she said in a strangled voice. 'This isn't fair!'

'Tough,' he said, and tipped her head back with a hard grip on her hair. His chin thrust out. 'So, do I have to carry you off to bed to get an answer?'

'You wouldn't—Holly's upstairs——'

'I have a very nice, large couch in my study down here,' he purred. 'Holly never comes into my study when the door is shut. This way——' He began to move with her, green eyes glittering. Cara pulled against him, floundering around in a maze of feeling and wants and fears. Mitch was suddenly forceful, determined, overriding her defences.

'I've never seen you like this——' she said, trying to prise his hand from her wrist as he pulled her relentlessly along.

'That's because I've only just realised what I want.' He manoeuvred her along the passageway to his study door. He reached for the handle.

'All right,' she said.

'All right, what?' Mitch yanked her close.

'I—can't face the idea of not seeing you again.'

Mitch's face softened into smiling lines. He cupped her face in one hand, dropped a kiss on her lips then flicked a hand against the door. 'It'll keep.'

'What will?' she asked, dazed.

'The couch.' He walked out to her car with her. 'Knowing you, you'll want a breathing space. I'll pick you up at seven on Wednesday night,' he added smoothly, opening the car door for her. Cara felt a prickle of alarm at that 'knowing you'. It was a vulnerable feeling to be so understood. She was annoyed, too, at this sudden, overweening masculine confidence. All she'd done was tell him she loved him and he was strutting about, coming on all masterful and taking over. Giving orders.

'Oh?' she queried.

'A party.'

'The one I refused on the grounds that it would be boring?'

'No, I gave that one a miss.' Mitch was unperturbed. 'This is a bit more formal, but I think you'll find some surprising people there.'

You for one, she thought, staring at him. Was he always like this when he'd decided he wanted something? Someone. Her. It was her that he wanted. Cara felt a rush of blood to her face and neck.

'Where will it be?' she asked.

He named an upmarket hotel. Cara's chin went up, her eyes sparkled. 'I don't think I have anything suitable to wear to a place like that,' she told him evenly. 'And the cost of repairing the Mini means I can't really afford to buy a new outfit.' She paused. 'Even if I wanted to.' She waited to see if he would repeat the mistake he'd made last time. Mitch held her gaze. His lower lip thrust out, then he smiled as if realising he'd just been challenged.

'Wear what you like, Cara.'

'I always do,' she warned.

He touched her cheek gently. 'You'll find something. After all, you lived in Paris for a year.'

Cara took this in with mixed feelings. 'All right, I'll come—on one condition.'

'What's that?'

'That you come to one of *my* parties.'

'Hell's bells!' Danny exclaimed when Cara emerged
from her bedroom on Wednesday night. 'I thought you
said you were going out with Kirby?'

'I am,' she said, and stopped in front of the mirror.
Perhaps she had overdone it. She flipped her plait
experimentally this way and that. She liked it—some
people might think it zany of course, but she liked it.
One side of her hair was cinched into the plait—the
other side was pure crimped, curling wilderness—a
sun-streaked honey-brown mass that sprang out
around her face and over one shoulder. She wore deep
pink baggy pants and an offbeat matching waistcoat
style top, fastened with plaited brass buttons and
fringed with tinkling camel bells. On her feet were
beaded, miniature-heeled sandals bought years ago in
a Moroccan market.

'What do you think?' She spun around, arms out.
The trousers ballooned, the bells jangled.

'The bells—the bells!' croaked Danny, hunching
over á la Quasimodo. She laughed and clipped his
arm.

'You look great. Where are you going?' he asked.
When she told him, he gave a long whistle. 'Won't you
look a bit—out of place?'

She shrugged. 'Probably.' Nothing was more
certain, she thought as she bound a rolled pink and
silver silk headband around her head. 'But Mitch
knows how I dress and I see no reason to change it.'

'That sounds like a challenge, Cara,' remarked
Danny. She didn't answer. It was true that she had
nothing to wear to Mitch's kind of dinner party. What
possible use would she have for satin or lace or elegant
little black dresses? Not that she hadn't been to
glamour affairs—she had. Once, she'd even attended

some millionaire's party on a yacht in the Greek
Islands—but pants and boob tube and a providential
satin shirt hadn't been out of place there because
although half the wealthy were flashing diamonds and
clanking gold chain, the other half looked like
beachcombers. Tonight though, she knew she was
deliberately emphasising her offbeat taste. Rather
confusedly she recognised her need to maintain her
individuality. Once he knew she loved him, Mitch had
evinced that sudden, spiralling confidence—and a
subtle new possessiveness that might be exciting but
struck a few warning notes too. She loved him, he
seemed to be saying, so it was only a matter of time
before she altered her ways and fitted in with his way
of life. Why, he had even hinted that she might have a
nice, acceptable little Paris gown hidden away in her
wardrobe. He seemed to feel that she could—and
would want to—wave some feminine magic wand and
come up with just the right look for the occasion.
Change herself to match him. And she didn't want to.
Danny was right, it *was* a challenge. This is *me*, she
was telling him. If you want me it has to be the way I
am. And if he decided he didn't want her the way she
was, then she could simply move on . . . she grimaced
at her reflection. A challenge, yes, but it was
cowardice too.

When she opened the door to Mitch he was smiling.
The smile died as he discovered her hair and bit by bit
discovered the waistcoat, the harem pants, the
sandals. His jaw clenched, there were sparks in his
eyes. He held out a boxed orchid—white with a blush
of pink in its throat.

'How fortunate that I chose the right colour,' he said
tautly.

'Come in while I put it on,' she said. She stood
before the mirror and tried the flower on her

waistcoat. It looked ridiculous. 'Oh, I know—in my hair—yes?'

She turned for his opinion, fascinated by the high colour in his cheeks, the angry white at the corners of his mouth.

'Perfect,' he snapped out, eyes on the plait and the curls and the headband. 'I knew there was *something* missing.'

Heart thumping wildly, Cara pinned the orchid in her hair. 'There.' She whirled around to him and he tilted his head with a puzzled air.

'What's that noise?'

'The bells—it's the bells!' Danny did his Hunchback of Notre Dame routine again, and Mitch looked more closely at Cara's outfit.

'Bells——' he said faintly, and closed his eyes for a moment. This was it, Cara thought. He would make some excuse not to go now. And that would be that. Her chin went up in anticipation. But he adjusted his bow tie, gave the edges of his dinner jacket a sort of 'girding for battle' snap and held out his arm to her.

'Sensational, Cara. I can guarantee every eye will be on you.'

He was right. Every eye *was* on her. From the moment she walked in on Mitch's arm she was the cynosure of all eyes. Cara didn't care about that. The other women were uniformly elegant—salon hair and glittering nails and stiletto heels, discreet glowing pearls and dazzling diamonds in tasteful twos and threes. Cleo was there, cool, groomed, exquisitely gowned in organza with a burst of feminine ruffles over one shoulder. Her tranquil air was momentarily shattered when she saw Cara. Surprise was followed by a bleakness, quickly disguised. She greeted them with serene charm and held her greying escort's arm as fondly as if it was Mitch's.

At dinner Cara and Mitch shared a table with several animated younger people and an old school friend of Mitch's. John Glasson and his wife Norma were friendly, interesting and interested. They were curious but unbothered by her offbeat appearance. Not the stuffy friends she had accused him of having. There were plenty of stuffed shirts there, of course— patronising lawyers full of their own importance, brittle wives conscious of their dignity and social standing who treated Cara coolly and Mitch with a sort of condescending pity. She caught snippets of conversation here and there—

'—fellow was so incensed he took off his shoe and hoisted it at the bench—can you believe it——?'

'—devil's got into Kirby? His wife had style, brilliant girl—where did he find *this* one?'

'Busker? Good lord——'

'—a looker though. Outré but tasty. Sly dog——'

'—so he gave him another six months for contempt. Said, "As you've thrown your footwear at me, sir, I'm throwing the book at you". Dry old devil——'

'—Arabian Nights. Poor old Mitchell—first his girl goes punk, now this——'

No. Cara didn't care about the amused glances, the patronising comments. What these people thought of her didn't matter to her. But she did care about Mitch. She hadn't asked and he hadn't mentioned that this was a professional dinner party. His colleagues were here, people with whom he worked, against whom he competed. People to whom his reputation mattered. And she felt a slight sense of regret that her image might in some way harm him, diminish him. Yet, would she alter herself to avoid that? Should she? Cara didn't know. The issue of individuality that had seemed so clear-cut became hazy, especially as Mitch himself treated her as if she was indeed dressed in some acceptable little Paris number. He never left her side, and carried her off with every appearance of enthusiasm to meet people.

Mitch, in fact, seemed determined that she meet everyone present—high court judges, magistrates, barristers. She glanced up at him once or twice as he swept her away to another group and each time he met her gaze with a flinty smile. After a whirl of introductions, they danced.

'So tell me, Cara,' he asked softly, 'are you bored with my stuffy friends?'

'They're not *all* stuffy,' she admitted. 'Some are quite fun.'

'Ah—you noticed,' he said with a touch of sarcasm.

'A lot of them feel sorry for you being with such an outré type who can't even wear the right gear. Your reputation might have suffered tonight. Does that bother you, Mitch?'

He pulled her closer, spoke tersely in her ear. 'I'll survive.'

'You could have kept a much lower profile,' she said. 'You didn't *have* to flaunt me in front of everyone here——'

'Oh, yes, I did,' he gritted between his teeth as he smiled for the benefit of other passing dancers. 'Because I've got your measure now, Cara. I'm not going to make it easy for you. Wear your fancy dress—trick yourself out in a G-string and tassels if you like—but I won't hide you away. Not because I don't care that people might snigger and think I'm crazy. In my profession a reputation is valuable and I *do* care. But I won't play you down, because that would give you the excuse you're waiting for to pack your bags and that bowler hat and run away.'

She felt vulnerable, as if he'd stripped away her defences.

'That's crazy,' she said, swallowing hard.

'You know it isn't,' he muttered, and held her close, blandly returning the stares of others. Only Cara felt his tension and knew how great an effort he was making. She felt oddly humbled.

Later she saw Cleo in the ladies' room. Side by side they stood at a giant mirror. Cleo repaired her lipstick, Cara combed the free portion of her hair. They smiled a polite greeting and sneaked a glance at each other which coincided. They made an ironic contrast. The groomed, fashionable woman who belonged in this ritzy atmosphere, who could talk shop with lawyers—for however inept Cleo might be with her god-daughter, she shone here in the world she had made her own. And the zany outsider—wrong hair, wrong clothes, wrong opinions.

Cleo gave a strained little laugh. 'You think you know someone so well—what they like, what they want, and then suddenly they——' She ran eyes over Cara's Arabian Nights outfit and tore a tissue from a wall dispenser. She blotted her lipstick. 'I always thought Mitch had taste!' The crushed tissue was hurled into a bin. Cleo bit her lip. 'I beg your pardon. I must have had too many champagne cocktails——'

With great poise she took her bag and left. Such a civilised woman. Basically nice, Cara thought. Maybe *too* nice. It might have done Cleo more good to be really nasty. She had played a waiting game for Mitch for a long time and now her hopes were being foiled by a woman in camel bells; she must really want to spit chips. Cara felt very sorry for her.

There was the zing of tension in the air as Cara and Mitch drove away from the hotel in silence. Mitch frowned and his hands were clenched on the steering wheel. When they were almost home to her flat it became too much for Cara. She gave a muffled, nervous giggle. Mitch glanced sombrely at her. She laughed outright.

'What?' he demanded.

'A G-string, you said,' she gurgled. 'I just remembered. A G-string!'

His face relaxed. He edged the Peugeot into the kerb outside her flat, switched off the ignition and leaned on the wheel. 'And tassels.' he reminded her with a slow, wicked smile. Then his gaze wandered down to her breasts and he reached out for her. Awkwardly he bridged the space between the seats. Musically she came into his arms.

'Oh, my God,' groaned Mitch, 'camel bells—I must be out of my mind! You sound like a camel caravan in the Sahara,' he groaned again, lightly nibbling at her right shoulder; Cara giggled.

'It shouldn't turn me on,' he said peevishly, tasting her skin with a delicate touch of his tongue. 'We used to have two goats who sounded like you—acted like you too. Nothing but trouble, those goats, bells jingling, I remember——'

'Was that when you were a kid?' She spluttered into laughter at her own pun. He didn't seem to hear, but drew back a bit to brush the back of a hand over the bells sewn in semi-circles beneath her breasts. 'Ridiculous,' he said hoarsely.

Cara caught her breath as his hands roamed, setting more than bells ringing, but after a few moments her laughter exploded again, more from the same curious accumulated nervousness, a sudden high, than from amusement.

'I wish you'd stop laughing,' he said in an injured tone. 'I'm making love to you!'

'Sorry,' she giggled, '—but, Mitch—I just—can't stop——' Slowly he unclasped the first brass button of the waistcoat. 'Once I get the giggles—I just—

can't——' And the second. She wore no bra and his fingertips slid over the upper slopes of her breasts. "—just can't——' The third button and the fourth, and a soft tremor of bells as Mitch pushed the waistcoat to each side.

'Can't what?' he prompted softly, shaping his hands to her.

'Can't stop,' she whispered.

He lowered her a little on the seat into the deepest shadow and as his head went to her breasts Cara had no desire to laugh at all. Her only desire was to hold him tight and feel his mouth tug at her. Ah! And his hands smooth her thighs. She moved beneath him, frustrated. Too many clothes ... her hands spread over his flanks, she couldn't hold him close enough.

'Cara!' he said fiercely, and shifted his weight. His elbow rammed backwards into the car's controls. The windscreen wipers began a frantic swiping across the window.

'Oh, blast——' He eased himself around to turn it off and the horn blatted. It sounded like a foghorn in the dead quiet street. 'Dammit!' he swore as the door of the flat opened and Pete looked out. Cara ducked low and fastened her clothes, her body on fire. Mitch eased himself across into his own seat again, muttering, 'There must be some reason why I'm doing this ... taking a bra-less slave girl to meet my colleagues.' He tucked in a loosened shirt-tail and accidentally bipped the horn again. 'And now here I am behaving like some lovesick adolescent—*necking*, for God's sake, in a car——' A tweak of his bow tie, a swift, restoring brush of his hand over his hair 'Well, the reason's obvious. I'm mad.'

'Mad?' she asked. 'As in angry?'

'Mad as in lost my marbles, nuts, diminished responsibility——' He drew a deep breath, held it a

moment, then let it out, slow and controlled. He
turned his head to Cara and looked at her seriously.
His dashboard digital clock silently signalled a new
minute. Mitch leaned over and tenderly tilted her
chin. 'I love you. So it must be madness.' He kissed
her—a lingering light caress that shafted right to the
depths of her. 'And I want you,' he added. 'But make
no mistake, I want you for ever.'

For ever. Cara drew away, eyes wide. Hard to
take—that vision of a future without him. Yet all the
hard lessons of her youth, her parents' slow, mutual
destruction, her brother's misery through two marriage attempts, made her shrink from for ever. To take
love and make ruins of it seemed to Cara worse than to
let love go. Or it always had. With Guy it had been
easy. Guy had been a kindred spirit; he'd lived for the
here and now and it had been fun and uncomplicated.
If she could have made a lifetime thing work with
anyone it would have been with him. But Mitch? He
was different, locked into a kind of life she didn't
really understand. The gap between them was
immense.

'Mitch——' she began, but he put a finger to her
lips.

'I know. It's too soon,' he said wryly. 'Let's get the
hurdles out of the way first.'

CHAPTER EIGHT

AND so they jumped hurdles. They saw each other often—ate together, danced, and in the lengthening evenings of late spring, strolled by the river holding hands. They sailed in Mitch's boat, too long unused, out to the islands of Moreton Bay—the clean sands of Peel Island, the old convict ruins of St Helena. And they talked. And talked.

On the sandhills of Moreton Island, breathlessly between toboggan rides down the slopes and dogged climbs back up again, 'There was a time,' Cara said, taking in his sunburned, sand-dusted face, his sleeveless tank top and red board shorts, 'when I thought you couldn't have been a kid.'

'Oh yes?'

'Mmmm. You used to drop money in my hat with that lordly air and that serious, burdened expression, and I decided that you'd been born adult and never skinned your knees or slushed around in mud or overflowing street gutters after a rainstorm——'

'Oho—couldn't keep me out of a good, gutsy, overflowing gutter. And my mother considered nominating me for the Guinness Book of Records for skinned knees. She kept the antiseptic cream and bandages in the kitchen right alongside the peanut butter. I was a real ruffian!'

'So you say,' she panted, dragging her toboggan up the dune. 'It was Little Lord Fauntleroy shirts and breeches and polished shoes and neat, combed hair, I'll bet.'

'Torn tee-shirts and faded jeans.'

'Then bugle lessons and riding lessons—jodhpurs and hacking jackets and gymkhanas——'

'Mucking out the stable of the family horse—one ancient steed called Speedy Gonzales. As he got older we just called him Gonzales——'

'—then army cadets and cricket and rugby——'

'Army cadets and rowing and Aussie Rules.'

'—straight "A"s and into Law at Uni——'

'It wasn't that easy,' Mitch assured her. 'I had to work hard for my "A"s, and I had two part-time jobs while I was at school.'

'What jobs?'

'I was a trolley-boy.' He laughed at her puzzlement. 'You know, supermarket trolleys. At shopping centres. People leave them all over the place and I used to round them up——'

They reached the top of the dune, panted for breath.

'What was the other job?' asked Cara.

'I drove a lift in my holidays.'

'A lift driver? Oh, tell me another!' she grinned, and stretched out on her toboggan, dug into the sand with her toes and was off down the slope with the silken swish of sand beneath and the rush of salt air on her face. And Mitch was beside her, racing downhill too.

'Second Floor—Manchester-Dress Materials-Haberdashery-Lingerie and lay-by-going down,' he shouted, 'first floor-Ladies' Fashions-shoes-Ladies' Restroom-to-the-right, Showroom-to-the-left——'

Cara tumbled over at the base of the dune, lay arms outstretched on the sand, laughing up at the sky. Mitch loomed against the blue. '—going down. Mind the step, madam.' He grinned down at her, and the sun poured on them and little trickles of sand whispered down the slope where they'd been. Cara reached up to touch Mitch's face.

'Why next to the peanut butter?' she asked, stroking

his jaw. 'A funny place to keep bandages.'

'All part of the treatment. I'd go to Mum trying to be brave, yesterday's knee scabs scraped off into two new, raw patches. Antiseptic cream, a bandage and a peanut butter sandwich.' He sighed in reminiscence. 'My favourite food, then—peanut butter. Guaranteed to make me forget my wounds.' He bent and kissed her caressingly, looked at her a long time. 'What can we do to make you forget yours, love?'

For now he knew about it all—the outward appearance of happy families preserved for people who didn't matter, the inner destructive core of love gone wrong—rare moments of joy that were reminders of how it could be if only compromise and co-operation had joined with love. Smiling up at him here on the pale, warm sand with the sky blue and the sunlight benign, Cara felt the old fears fading. History didn't have to repeat itself. She reached up and pulled him down to her.

Mitch's work intervened, of course, in this new era. He still jumped to attention at the summons of his watch and mildly refuted all Cara's accusations that he let his work regiment his life. He would smile and put his arm around her.

'It just seems that way to you, love, because you've been living on the fringes so long. We have a lot of time for fun.'

And sometimes Cara would argue that her life-style was not merely on the fringes of his but a legitimate, wonderful way to live—one that he too should try now and then, and sometimes with his arm around her and the glow of contentment within her just from being with him, she would let it pass.

The weather grew hot and humid—hazed mornings and sweltering middays and stormy evenings when the heat was briefly relieved by rain. But the cool moisture of the night became the humid torment of the following day. Mrs Leslie, Mitch's housekeeper, back in action again, predicted a scorching Christmas. She was a bustling cottage-loaf of a woman who serenely accepted Cara's occasional presence and chatted on and on about the weather and her new grandson. Little Denzil, six weeks old, was already *months* ahead of most babies his age. If only his daddy had a job and they could afford a few more things for the little chap, she lamented.

Pete, who had received no answering letter yet from Vivian, sank deeper into gloom. 'I should have proposed sooner,' he kept saying. 'Now she probably *has* met some big, blond Swede—she'll probably tear up my letter and laugh,' he brooded. 'Sven. I'll bet his name's Sven. Damned Swedes——' So he counted the days since his mailed proposal, Danny counted the days until he would have Samantha back again and Cara—Cara counted nothing at all. Her habitual happiness had intensified around her—a beautiful haze, an insular haze that shut out occasional nagging, warning voices. She taught at the Academy and played her music and let her instincts take her closer and closer still to Mitch, felt herself drawn into his life. His and Holly's.

Early one evening while Pete was still fulminating over the hypothetical Sven who was almost certainly using his heartless Nordic charm on Vivian, Viv herself arrived. Pete opened the door and found his beloved surrounded by packs and duffle bags. Viv was pale from jet lag and didn't even say hello. She threw her arms around Pete and said, 'Yes, you big ox—I *will* marry you.'

There had to be a party. They figured that if Viv, staying with her sister, slept all the next day and half of Saturday, she might be fit to celebrate on Saturday night. It would be a jumping affair—Pete's artist and student friends, Viv's sister who was a history lecturer, her Aunt Phoebe who had done the odd spot of 'exotic dancing' in her chequered past, some mutual musician friends of Danny's and Pete's——

'—Uni students, and of course Arty the fire-eater——' Cara finished telling Mitch as they walked that evening along the aviary path in his garden. 'You can't say no. It was part of the deal that you come to my kind of party.'

He laughed. 'It sounds different.'

'It will be,'she promised. 'As different from that party you took me to as Bach is from the Beatles.' A faint, uncomfortable sensation accompanied the words. 'Bring Holly if you like. She could sleep in my room when she's tired.'

'No.'

'Not the right kind of people for her to mix with?' Cara asked with a touch of asperity. Mitch turned her to him, pulled her into his arms.

'Don't jump to conclusions. Holly has plans to spend the weekend with her best friend's family,' he said and he kissed her a little roughly.

'Dad—Grandma and Grandpa are here!' Holly called, and the bamboo rustled as she came along the path, in advance of the visitors. 'And *Cleo*.' Tall, thin Justice Holley, silver-haired and browed, followed his diminutive wife whose dark hair was frosted with grey. Behind them was Cleo. She had remained an intimate of her best friend's parents, it seemed. Cara couldn't decide why that jarred a little.

They strolled into the aviary courtyard, an elegant trio—the Judge tweedy, smoking a pipe, Mrs Holley trim in green linen and Cleo elegant in a white trouser suit. She wore a look of transparent delight as she looked around. Until she saw Cara.

There was a short exchange of restrained greeting. Mrs Holley laid her hands on Mitch's arms and turned her cheek for his kiss. She herself gave one of those social little kisses that landed mid-air, but there was genuine affection in it, Cara saw. The Judge chomped hard on his pipe and shook hands. 'Good to see you, Mitchell.'

Cleo kissed Mitch on the cheek in a sisterly fashion, though her hand lingered a moment too long on his arm.

Cara stood by the aviary and watched, feeling like a visitor from outer space in an old, long skirt and a collarless, cotton shirt hung about with belts. Her hair was a great, untamed mass and her face was bare of make-up. When Mitch drew her forward to introduce her to his in-laws she fancied there was a faint dubiousness in his manner. His eyes ran over her as if the presence of others had suddenly thrown her into unflattering contrast.

The two older people gave polite smiles, but Cara felt that it was only a lifetime of good manners that prevented them from demanding outright why he should be involved with such a gypsy. Their resentment that Mitch might even consider her in their daughter's place was firmly controlled but there, in the air.

'Holly tells us you're a flautist, Miss Matheson,' the Judge said, chewing out the words around the stem of his pipe. Cara smiled, trying to imagine Holly using the term, but obligingly talked about her flute playing. She was as matter-of-fact about her occasional short seasons with reputable symphony orchestras as she was about her teaching and busking. The conversation curled this way and that, as quiet and subtle as the Judge's pipe smoke. Holly went into the aviary to replace the water, using the tap installed inside for that purpose, and there was some discussion on the birds.

'Snowy looks wonderful,' said Mrs Holley, waggling her fingers through the mesh at the sulphur-crested cockatoo. 'I'm glad. He was always Fran's favourite—here, boy——' The cockatoo came over and gently nibbled on her finger. Cleo too cooed at the bird.

'Hello there, Snowy—who's a good boy, then?' she said.

Not Snowy apparently. He sidewalked along the mesh to Cleo and gave a quick, vicious nip at her fingers. With a little cry Cleo pulled her hand out of the cage. Her perpetually pleasant expression faltered. In fact, she glared at the cockatoo.

'Why, you——' She nursed her finger and valiantly quashed the alternative names she might have had in mind for Snowy. 'I must have startled him,' she said with commendable restraint, and took Mitch's proffered handkerchief to wrap around the finger that was bleeding now. Cara frowned. Did the woman always repress her natural emotions? It was true she had revealed herself to Cara at the hotel that night, but very briefly. No sooner had she opened the door on her feelings than she slammed it shut again. Had she spent all her youth smiling graciously, the good loser as her best friend romped off with the trophies and the honours?

'I'm sorry about that, Cleo,' Mitch apologised. 'Snowy isn't usually nasty.'

'I've never known him to bite,' said Mrs Holley, 'or any of the others, come to think of it. I don't think Fran ever had a nip from a bird—and you know how many she had over the years, Cleo—ever since you were at school together she kept birds. Of course, she always had a way with creatures of any kind. Dogs

used to follow her home—and she could do anything
with cats.'

'And horses,' the Judge said.

'Oh yes. Horses. I don't think there was a horse she
couldn't handle—what a rider she was—you remember, Cleo?'

Cleo smiled and said she did. And bound up her
finger with Mitch's handkerchief. And bound it. And
bound it.

'—even the most vicious animal would never bite
Fran——' Mrs Holley collected herself as if realising
this reminiscence was not in the best of taste. She went
to Cleo's side. 'Not too bad, is it, my dear?'

'No, it's fine.' Cleo smiled. But the handkerchief
was wrapped tight around her hand. Cara couldn't
help thinking that if it was somebody's neck, the
charge would be strangulation. Poor Cleo. Bound to be
bitten. So nice, but trying too hard for all the wrong
reasons. Children and animals seemed to sense it.

'Are you a bird fancier, Miss Matheson?' enquired
the Judge.

'Yes, I am. But I fancy mine in the wild.'

He considered her through his pipe smoke. 'Not an
animal liberationist, are you?' he smiled faintly.

'In as far as I dislike caged animals, I suppose I am,'
she said, refusing to be intimidated by the man's soft-
spoken superiority. 'These beautiful creatures
shouldn't be locked up; they should be free.'

There was a very vague bristling.

'As Cara told me the first time she saw them,' Mitch
commented drily. 'You'll find that Cara always speaks
her mind,' he told his in-laws, and there was a further
bristling, whether at the inference that they would be
seeing more of her, or at her outspokenness, it was
hard to know.

'Mmmm,' said Mrs Holley with a dutiful smile. 'How refreshing.'

'But, Cara——' Holly was in the aviary still and came over to look out, her hands spread on the mesh. 'This isn't just an ordinary cage—I mean it isn't as if the birds are stuck in those awful little things people keep canaries and budgies in. This is a beautiful cage—it has a tree and grass and plants growing in it, just like outside.'

'But it *isn't* outside, is it, Holly?' she said softly. 'You're in there with them—take a look around.' Cara glanced at Cleo, still nursing her injured finger. 'It's big and it's pretty and it seems to have everything, but how long do you think it would be before you got tired of walking about in that same space with the same tree, the same grass——'

Holly took her hands from the mesh and turned about, looked up at the birds on the tree's branches and the mesh roof that kept them from the highest limbs. Snowy flew up and perched, raised his sulphur crest and tilted his head to one side to watch them all.

'Did you know cockatoos can live to be a hundred?' Holly said rather irrelevantly after a while.

'How old is he now?'

The girl chewed her lip. 'Ten,' she said at last, and they all looked up at the beautiful bird. The words were left unsaid. Only ninety years to go.

'It's very interesting—this bleeding heart view about animal captivity,' the Judge mulled over it a bit, 'but of course it really isn't valid when the creatures are bred in captivity. The extremists might advocate releasing creatures that wouldn't have any idea of survival in their natural state. Most wouldn't last a week. But of course, that's idealism for you.'

'I think the idealists' question might be—is a century of security better than a week of freedom,' said Mitch with a wry look at Cara. 'Wouldn't it?'

'I don't know,' she replied levelly, aware that her intransigent stance had annoyed him. But Mitch must know that she could not trim her feelings to suit. 'But I suppose my question is—why are they bred in captivity at all?'

Only a puff of pipe smoke answered this. Holly emerged from the cage and shot the two bolts on the door. They all walked away along the jungle path. Cara took a last look back at the aviary and its inhabitants and she felt a sudden sense of depression. Cleo, too, looked back and for a moment Cara saw frustration, even hatred there. She caught Cara's eye and smiled. The door was shut again, and locked. As the bamboo rustled and swayed behind them along the path, Cara heard a single screech from the cage.

Viv and Pete's engagement party rocketed from infancy to adolescence in thirty minutes.

'I *knew* she'd snap me up,' yelled Pete smugly over the blast of Stevie Wonder. 'Never had a moment's doubt.'

Danny and Cara exchanged glazed glances. They hadn't been able to decide which was worse—Pete's morbid anxieties that Viv might reject him, or his cockiness since she had flown half-way across the world to say yes. Viv winked at Cara, who'd told her of Pete's imaginary Nordic nemesis.

'I would have been here even sooner,' she said, 'if it hadn't been for Sven.' It wiped Pete's grin clean away. Temporarily anyway.

It became impossible to hear guests knocking at the door, so they simply left it open, and Cara's eyes and ears were fine-tuned for the sight and sound of Mitch. Here, surrounded by her friends, she was restless, eager for him. Concealing her impatience, she

welcomed some newcomers, turning her back on the
door for a few moments. There was a funny little hush
against the steady thump of Danny's stereo speakers.
As heads turned, Cara looked around.

Mitch was there, tall and distinguished and framed
beautifully in the open door, carrying a bottle of
champagne and a giant red-ribbon-wrapped box of
chocolates.

He wore a dinner suit.

Frilled shirt.

Cummerbund.

Bow tie.

Cara's lit-up smile faded bit by bit as she looked him
over from his gleaming, dark groomed hair—freshly
cut for the occasion by the look of it—to his gleaming,
speckless black shoes.

'Good God, I didn't know it was fancy dress!' a man
quipped behind Cara. 'Blimey, I think it's one of the
Royals——' someone else said. The crowd began
buzzing again. Cara flushed a little. She hadn't
realised until now just how much she'd wanted her
friends to like Mitch, to see in him what she herself
saw. And by turning up like this he'd set himself apart
from them. And of course, it was just what she had
done that other night. Had he felt like this, then, when
he found out that she had not been prepared to make
any concessions to please him? She looked him
straight in the eye.

'Touché, Mitch.'

He smiled and walked in, unblinkingly put his
bottle of champers—French and the real thing—on
the table with the cardboard wine casks, and
presented the chocolates to an astonished Viv. Cara
introduced him around and he nodded and smiled and
looked very pleasant but stiff as if trying to hide his
boredom. So soon. Cara's heart sank. A few of her

friends, not so hamstrung by convention as his, made open remarks about his clothes. 'Did you get lost on the way to the Savoy, mate?'

Mitch met Cara's eyes in amusement.

'I always wear what I like,' he said, using her own words.

'A matter of personal integrity, Mitch?'

'Oh, definitely. I knew you, of all people, would understand that.'

She felt all twisted up. Hoist with her own petard, she couldn't complain. And now she could appreciate just how difficult it had been for him that other night—more difficult than this could ever be with her free and easy friends.

'Sure,' she said. 'It's live and let live with my friends, Mitch. They might think you a little pretentious at first——'

He opened his eyes wide. 'No!'

'—but they'll take you as they find you. If they like you it wouldn't matter if you wore a Superman suit.'

He laughed. Cara worried at it and realised why this bothered her so. She'd felt the need to make a statement by dressing as she had. 'I refuse to get lost in your world', that was what she had been saying. But for Mitch this was just a joke—an unexpected display of humour to pay her back. Mitch was making no statement; why should he? There was no danger of him ever getting lost in her world.

'You look wonderful, Cara,' he said in a low voice, and his eyes roamed over her blue dress. It was thin cotton jersey and slim with a wide neckline that slipped tipsily off one shoulder. He leaned closer so that his mouth was almost touching the bare skin. 'Is there anyone in your room?' he murmured.

'No.'

'Good.' He took her arm in a masterful grip and

swung her into the short passageway, opened the
bedroom door and whisked her through it. It was
dark, but Mitch didn't bother turning on the light.
When he'd shut the door he pulled her into his arms
and found her bare shoulder with his mouth.
'Mmmmm—all through those introductions I was
glassy-eyed wondering how I could get you alone——'

'I thought it was because you were bored.'

'Could anyone be bored around you?' he asked
huskily, dragging his mouth along the side of her neck
to her ear. 'You're life itself.'

His kiss was fierce, hungry, and she matched him in
fierceness and hunger. The stereo bass beat vibrated
the floor and the walls around them. The darkness
danced with rhythm and brilliant bursts of colour.
Mitch hauled her close and Cara wrapped her arms
tight about his waist. Then in tacit agreement, they
stilled, standing there, arms around each other, letting
desire diminish for the moment.

'Won't you be hot in that ridiculous outfit?' she said.

'Possibly. Do you want me to take it off?'

'Not all of it.' She reached for his bow tie, tugged at
it gently.

'Pete poses nude for sculptors; Aunt Phoebe was a
stripper—your friends could take it.'

'But I might not be able to.' The tie came loose
silkily in her hands. She unfastened the top button of
his frilled shirt, then the second.

'This isn't right, you know,' he said as he removed
his jacket. 'I should be in a phone booth.'

'Why?'

He put his mouth to her ear and whispered, 'I'm
wearing a Superman suit under this.'

It was a super party. Viv, looking bleary-eyed again,
danced non-stop in Pete's arms whether there was
music or not. Rhonda, who had agreed to come, with

some trepidation, as this was her first social event since her blindness, was there, and surprised to discover that she didn't need to see to dance. Arty the fire-eater was there, taking more conventional refreshment and plenty of it, and Viv's Aunt Phoebe, former 'exotic dancer', kept up her end of a spirited debate on the sexual exploitation of women and to Viv's relief, kept all her clothes on. Miss Vernon made a brief appearance before her hay fever suddenly manifested itself. Her sniffles accelerated into sneezes and after she'd stunned the party with the force of the first, she scuttled off upstairs where she could be heard 'Ya-hoo'ing even over the princely efforts of Mick Jagger and friends.

The rogue fluorescent, swathed in red cellophane, gave out with its disco effects and the dining table, laden under French sticks and cheese and mounds of Mario's half-price fruit and veg, gradually lightened. Mitch, sleeves rolled up, shirt opened half-way down his chest, talked politics here, art there. He danced Greek style to Danny's bouzouki, stumbling along good-naturedly, following Cara's lead. He looked unbelievably sexy, Cara thought, hard pressed to keep her eyes off him.

By one o'clock the numbers had thinned to less than half. Several of the guests were asleep. Viv was zonked out on Cara's bed and Pete had joined her.

'I don't know where I'm going to sleep tonight,' Cara joked, and turned to meet Mitch's eyes.

'Sleep with me,' he said softly, very softly. She swallowed.

'Mitch—I——'

'All right then,' he amended. 'Swim with me.'

'Swim? At this hour?'

'Too unconventional for you, Miss Matheson?

After busking in Paris and hoodwinking the tourists in Greece?'

She smiled. Swim with him? It was all the same. If she went with him now she would end the night in his arms. He took her hand. 'Bring a swimsuit if you want.'

But she didn't.

The pool shimmered in its own underwater light. A single lamp glowed in the garden, holding back the jungle that swept around from the aviary and the side of the house. In the air was an early morning hush—no breeze, no movement. Just stillness and waterglow and moon-cast shadows. Across the vast, dark sky stars were scattered like notes of a theme too grand to be played.

They sat on cushioned sun-loungers and drank some wine, looking at each other until the night's still intensity gathered around them, shrinking the great skyscape to spangled intimacy. The silence was pierced by a harsh cry. Cara laughed, relieved to break the tension. 'The peacock?'

Mitch nodded.

'Where do peacocks go at night?' she asked, a high, nervous note in her voice.

'This one has a shelter, but usually prefers its favourite place in the garden——'

'Oh.'

Mitch cleared his throat. 'Did you know that they breed wild in some places in Australia?'

'No.'

'The species is of course, introduced. But there are bush areas where a pair have escaped and started colonies. On Rottnest Island just off the coast near Perth.' He paused. 'Have you been to Western Australia?'

A bubble of laughter rose in her. Mitch was nervous too. Gravely she said she had not been to Western Australia. She looked at him. He looked at her and their laughter burst out suddenly, was sustained a while on the still air, then stopped. Cara stood up and reached for her zip. Eyes on Mitch, she slipped off her dress. He rose and unbuttoned his shirt, tossed it on the ground, then reached for his trouser zip. But he paused a moment, eyes on Cara as she removed her briefs and stood naked in the moonlight. He drew in his breath sharply, uttered a muffled curse as he tried to hurry. When she laughed he shot her a fizzing look.

'Last one in's a dirty rat,' she giggled, feeling as if all the wine had rushed to her head. A glorious feeling of power gripped her. She put her hands on her hips and gave a provocative shimmy. 'Remember that time you caught me doing the Charleston?' she said, pouting her lips. 'Ooh-boop-a-doop!' She turned around, wiggled her behind. Mitch tripped over his trousers and stumbled. And swore.

Cara laughed headily, ran to the pool edge and poised there a moment where the underwater light caught at her. There was an eloquent groan from Mitch, then the sound of his shoes urgently hitting the ground. She dived. Two splashing lengths of the pool later he caught her from behind, his hands slithering over her midriff and belly.

'It took you long enough,' she gasped, turning in his arms.

'I hope you'll tell me that again later,' he growled, and pulled her close. Their mouths touched and the water's coolness on their lips bubbled into warmth. In slow motion they explored each other, languorously in dreamlike certainty that there was time—and time—to savour each new touch, each new barrier surmounted. Eyes closed, Cara drew Mitch in her mind from touch—the curve of his head sweeping down here to neck and shoulders, lean muscled and wide. Her fingertips found the bony hollows just above the tangle of wet hair on his chest. It had a pleasing roughness, that hair, contrasted with smooth skin that covered his back right down to . . . 'Mmmm,' Mitch murmured into her neck. His thighs were rough with hair too, and her trailing hands felt their power—such beautiful male lines . . . eyes closed, she drew her picture of him, and Mitch's body leapt between her hands. He splashed backwards as if he'd been struck by lightning.

'Shocked?' she taunted, and lifted her arms to the moon in a few lazy backstrokes. He caught her, one arm beneath her as she floated on the surface—and held her there to trace a tender, meandering line from her temple down her cheek. He gathered up palmfuls of water and trickled them over her breasts so that the pale skin tautened, glistened in the moonlight. Then he bent to taste and together they sank into the milky aqua depths.

The peacock cried again as they went, wrapped in towels, into the house. On deep, soft carpet they made their way into Mitch's study. Cara was glad he hadn't taken her to a bedroom; the bedrooms here belonged to Fran. The floor-length windows framed a part of the jungle garden. Moonlight lay silver along palm leaves, lifting them from inky shadows. So high were the trees and vines that only a saucer of sky was visible. A star sparkled in it.

With a smile Mitch unplugged the telex and the phone. He led her to a massive couch thrown with cushions.

'I told you it would wait,' he said, and drew her down.

CHAPTER NINE

THEY woke as they had that other time on the mountain. Face to face, Mitch's arm about her waist, her hand curved over his shoulder.

'Hello,' he murmured.

'Mmmmm,' she said and, stretch against him, kissed him. 'Mmmmm,' she said again with a satisfied, reminiscent smile. Mitch grinned, raised himself on one elbow.

'Do I take it we're compatible in bed?'

'Such fake modesty! You know the answer to that.' Idly Cara toyed with the hair over his forehead, ran a fingertip along each eyebrow. 'Will you make the coffee or shall I?'

'You want it now, my sweet?' He arched a brow at her.

'Yes, please. I always like coffee first thing in the morning.'

'And what do you like second?' he murmured against her neck.

'I'll tell you after the coffee.'

He laughed and got up to wrap the towel around his waist.

'You have smashing legs,' Cara observed, hitching herself on to her elbows to watch him. Mitch struck a pose that showed off his legs. There was a scream from outside. The peacock strutted from a flattened bower in the garden right outside the uncurtained window. It looked in, apparently unimpressed with Mitch's legs.

He laughed. 'You did want to know where peacocks

went at night. A good thing the damned thing can't talk.'

He went away and came back later with a tray of coffee and croissants, and they sat on the couch in the companionable intimacy of lovers to talk and laugh and let their eyes linger on each other, their hands reach out to touch. It seemed natural to share a breakfast like this in his book-lined study with all his tyrannical gadgets mute for once. He wasn't even wearing Superwatch. He wasn't wearing anything at all. Neither was she.

'Just one drawback to all this,' Mitch said, dusting himself off. 'Croissant crumbs.' He reached over to remove a flake of pastry from Cara's forearm, then with a quick, wicked glance bent instead and licked it off. She giggled. With the tip of her tongue she delicately removed several crumbs from his chest where they clung in the rough and springy hair. It was funny but amazingly sensual. Her body stirred, her pulses beat a tattoo of anticipation.

'On the other hand, crumbs in bed aren't so bad— mmmmm.' Mitch licked up a particle from the slope of her breast, another imaginary one from the tip. He was thorough, and Cara arched and twisted in pleasure. She sank her fingers into his hair as his head moved down over her midriff. 'Delicious,' he growled. 'You had jam——' And his mouth sought the sweetness until Cara was wild with hunger and imploring, but it was just the beginning and it was her turn to play and to tease and taste and his turn to hunger and implore before they came together—he slipping into her, she closing around him in perfect union.

Later they walked outside and the Sunday morning hush lapped around them. Mitch caught her hand as they walked beneath the twining grape leaves on the

patio where she had played her flute a lifetime ago.
The shadows flickered over them—vine laterals hung
down, tendrils reaching, swaying.

'Marry me, Cara.'

And the moment, like so many others with Mitch,
seemed absolute—with their loving so new and real,
with sun dappling them and a timeless quiet and
insect buzz and for ever stretching out ahead like some
sleepy paradise.

'Yes,' she said.

Later Cara realised she should have known that that
one 'yes', would change everything. It released a storm
of energy into sleepy paradise. Pete congratulated and
cautioned and Danny sighed and wished her happy
without much conviction, and Miss Vernon upstairs,
whose great love had married someone else twenty
years ago, thought it was lovely. Just—'Yahoo!'—
lovely. Mr Strachan nobly ignored her gladiator
sandals and fawned on the future Mrs Kirby, and her
fellow teachers gave her sidelong looks and stopped
telling jokes about the administration in the lunch
room. Holly's reaction was startled, delighted.

'Can I be a bridesmaid?' she asked. 'Wait until my
hair's grown before you get married.'

Mrs Leslie thought it was marvellous, and the
Holleys disguised their amazement and disappointment and were exceptionally good-mannered about it.
Cara wondered what Cleo would make of it. She felt
very uneasy about Cleo, but there wasn't time to dwell
on it. Being engaged entailed so many things. The
ring, for instance—for Mitch had insisted on a ring.

'We'll do this properly,' he'd said, and whisked her
off to a prestige jewellers where they argued over a
magnificent diamond cluster that Mitch favoured and
a simple sapphire.

The assistant was on the side of the diamonds,

naturally enough—it had almost as many noughts on
the price as stones in the cluster, and if he thought it
odd that a girl in cheesecloth and sandals should resist
such a treasure, he covered up well. Cara glared at
Mitch when he took her hand and tried to slip the
diamond ring on for the second time.

'Mitch, I'm only agreeing to a ring at all because you
want me to have one. I don't *need* the symbolism. I
know how I feel in *here*.' She tapped her heart and the
assistant discreetly discovered a need to buff up a
silver platter behind him. 'I will *not* wear that—that
chandelier on my finger!'

'I want the best for you——'

'I've got the best,' she said softly, touching his face.
'If you must buy me a ring—make it one that says "I
love you", not one that shouts, "Look at me!" '

He chuckled and returned the diamond cluster to
the attendant, who turned with immaculate timing
from his buffing to receive the ring. 'We'll take the
sapphire,' Mitch said to him. 'It's sincere. That one is
just an exhibitionist.'

The world had to be told. Cara had to meet Mitch's
partners, have a drink at the home of his friends John
and Norma Glasson.

The Holleys very graciously invited them to
dinner—a tacit acceptance of what must be. They did
not want to be cut off from their only grandchild, so
they would make the best of the situation and try to get
along with Mitch's new wife-to-be. Mitch's club had a
ladies' night soon, and she had to go to that too; Cara
reluctantly conceded that camel bells and Indian
muslin were now redundant. Mitch went shopping
with her, enthusing when she regarded herself
dubiously in elegant clothes.

'Cara, love, you look more beautiful than ever,' he
said, eyes glowing at crystal blue silk.

'God, that demure look is so *sexy* on you,' he growled at a slim skirt and jacket in cream with a hip-tied burgundy shirt.

'Grrrrr,' to a strapless midnight blue gown, clinging to the hips, swinging full and soft almost to her ankles. And Cara surveyed this stranger in fine clothes and had her doubts, but she wasn't proof against Mitch's admiration and the glow of pride in his eyes. He went with her to a shoe store where she tried elegant courts with tall, slim heels and strappy evening shoes with taller, slimmer heels. Her feet, accustomed to the freedom of sandals, seemed imprisoned in the glamour shoes, and as she staggered from one pair to another she tossed him a baleful look.

'I wouldn't do this for anyone else, you know.'

And Mitch grinned—almost purred in satisfaction. 'I know,' he said.

Under the bemused gaze of Danny and Pete and Viv she practised walking in her heels until her wobbles were barely noticeable, and she went out to the cocktail parties and dinners in her new finery and found that for Mitch's sake she could temper some of her uncompromising honesty, and if it hurt a little bit now and then to hold her tongue in diplomacy rather than to speak her mind, she had only to look at Mitch to ease the pain. What Mitch thought and felt mattered more than these others, and he was at first startled, then humbled, then transparently delighted that she would make these concessions for him. In private she was as direct and frank as ever and he found the contrast intriguing.

'I think I'm loving you more every day,' he said once. 'I didn't think it was possible.'

Holly couldn't seem to make up her mind about this new official relationship. From initial elation she gradually withdrew a little as if she feared she might

suddenly be left on the outside. All the warmth and
love that Cara brought to bear couldn't change that,
and she realised that the problem was rooted in
insecurity. Holly, fearing that she had not been
wanted, would always be wary and jealous of her
father's love. Cara was convinced that Cleo herself
might have unwittingly planted the disquieting ideas
in Holly's mind, but how to remove the doubts?

They ran into Cleo at Mitch's club dinner. He had
already broken the news of the engagement to her by
phone, Mitch told Cara—as an old friend of the family
she warranted advance notification. She had been
delighted, he said. Cleo repeated her delight on this
occasion, but Cara noticed how tightly she held her
purse, how forced was her charming smile. Cleo's last
hopes of stepping into Fran's shoes were fading and
she knew it.

Later Cara saw her in the powder room, not quite by
accident, she thought. Cleo had followed her, and
when two other women had left the mirrors, her public
face sagged. She looked at Cara in bafflement as if
wondering how she had lost to such a one. How unfair
it must seem when she had tried so hard, invested so
much time in being useful to Mitch.

'How long do you think you can keep it up?' She
gestured with her lipstick at Cara's new image. 'Won't
you miss the camel bells and your—tattooed friends?'

'They still have their place,' said Cara, unable
somehow to take offence. Cleo's spite seemed oddly
ineffectual, as if she hadn't had much practice.

'Isn't that a bit naive?' she said with a high laugh.
'Mitchell is a man going places—he won't want your
vagabond friends foisted on to him. He should be
marrying someone who understands his career,
someone who fits in, who could care for him and his
home and his daughter——'

'Someone like you?' asked Cara gently. How much
had it cost Cleo, she wondered, in terms of her own
career, her own personal life, to try to make herself
Fran's replacement?

'I belong in his world. You don't. I give you six
months and then he'll see——'

Cara shook her head. 'Haven't you wasted enough
time, Cleo? You could have made something of your
life instead of trailing along in Fran's wake——'

'I don't know what you mean.'

'You do. She had brains and beauty and popularity
and classy parents and money. A best friend like that
can be a hard act to follow.'

Cleo looked at herself in the mirror. 'I could never
keep up,' she said almost to herself. 'She did
everything better than me. She had everything and I
had nothing.'

Nothing. How sad. First she'd been popular Fran
Holley's best friend, then beautiful Fran's bridesmaid,
then godmother to the brilliant barrister Fran Kirby's
child. Unable to compete, merely complement, her
identity tied up with her best friend's prestige and
achievements. And now, when there was no need to
compete at last, when she thought she could step into
the starring role and inherit Fran's child and her
husband and, in a way, her classy parents—she was
thwarted.

'Make a new life, Cleo,' Cara urged. 'You don't love
Mitch. You want him because you've always wanted
what Fran had. You have brains and talents of your
own—why don't you stop feeling ashamed and admit
you hated her sometimes? You must have wanted to
be rotten to her now and then instead of nice and
gracious. It isn't anything unnatural——' Cara hesitated to go on, feeling the irony that it had to be *her* of
all people to whom Cleo had opened up. 'You've

locked up your real feelings for so long that you might
as well be a—a prisoner. Like one of Fran's birds in
that cage.' Cleo looked down, touched the small
plaster on her finger where Snowy had bitten her.
'Why don't you break free, Cleo, before Fran hurts
you any more?'

The woman's eyes widened. For a moment tears
sparkled in them. But she raised her chin, leaned over
to the mirror and flicked at her cheeks and her hair
with studied casualness.

'I really don't know what you're talking about,' she
said. 'Tell me—is the wedding to be a civil affair or
church?'

'Church,' said Cara softly, 'I wouldn't feel married
any other way.'

'Church.' Cleo's mouth trembled. 'Yes, I always
thought——'

'Cleo,' Cara said with compassion. 'I'm sorry——'

'Don't you dare feel sorry for me!' Cleo almost
hissed, and left with great dignity.

Cara asked Mitch about Cleo on the way home.

'Have you and Cleo ever been—more than friends?'

He looked amused. 'Cleo was marvellous after the
accident—took over things that I just couldn't face.
She's always been willing to partner me to dinners and
things like that soirée to save me from do-gooding
matchmakers who can't bear to see a man
unattached.'

'But there was never any—romance between you?'

He stopped the car and leaned over to her, cupping
the side of her face in his hand. He was smiling.

'You're jealous.'

'No, I'm not——'

He kissed her mouth and chuckled. 'Jealous.' He
found the idea extremely pleasing. 'No need. Cleo is
Holly's godmother and a good friend. There's never

been any question of anything else.' Then he pulled
her close and kissed her, and before she was totally
distracted she couldn't help wondering what problems
lay ahead if Cleo continued to call around as a fond
godmother hoping for a disintegration of Mitch's
marriage, and Holly herself remained insecure.

Holly's fears crystallised in the question she asked
Cara next evening.

'Will you and Dad have babies?'

Cara laughed foolishly. 'We haven't actually talked
about that, but—oh yes, I think we'll have babies.' She
could almost see Holly's envy of the babies to come.

'My mother never meant to have children. She
always said that. She wanted a career.'

'You heard that from your godmother, I suppose—
your unimpeachable source? But Holly, she was
repeating what your mother said as a schoolgirl and
student. Lots of women say that and then they meet a
man and fall in love and suddenly having children
seems like a wonderful thing——'

'She was always working. She used to go away a lot.'

'She was a woman who needed the challenge of her
work, I suppose. But she spent time with you when she
could, didn't she?'

'We always used to feed the birds together——'
Holly said distantly, then, 'the new baby would have
wrecked her practice. I overheard one of Dad's friends
say so——'

Cara sighed. On such tiny things, massive fears
grew.

'Not necessarily. And I'm sure she thought a new
baby worth that risk anyway. Ask your father. He'll
tell you it's so.'

'Will he?' Holly said in a small voice, and Cara saw
that it was a Catch-22 situation. She didn't want to
believe it, but she didn't want to ask in case her fears

were confirmed. Meanwhile the doubt was as destructive as the actuality would be.

It was Kay Leslie who was instrumental in
removing that doubt. The housekeeper confided
further about little Denzil's progress and her son-in-
law's desperate financial plight and how awful it was
that they didn't even have a car carry-cot for the baby,
which was very dangerous. Cara relayed this to Mitch
who said he would arrange for Mrs Leslie to have a
Christmas bonus which would pay for a carry-cot for
her grandson.

'And there are some things stored away under the
stairs that she could have—I daresay it's all in good
condition still.'

'What things?'

'The stuff Fran bought for the baby. I should have
given it away long ago, but I couldn't face sorting it
out.'

Cara grabbed his arm. 'So it's still there? Has Holly
ever seen it?'

He looked puzzled at her vehemence. 'I doubt it. I'll
tell Kay where it is and——'

'No, no.' Cara chewed her lip. 'I'll find it. I'll get
Holly to help me.'

It wasn't easy. Holly was secluded with a blasting
long-play of the Pointer Sisters, but Cara planted the
notion of a treasure-hunt-style search in the spare
room and left. Five minutes later Holly joined her.

'What are we looking for?' she asked Cara.

'Just some things your Dad wants to give to Mrs
Leslie for her new grandson.'

'Oh, *my* old stuff,' said Holly, 'That's a bit ancient,
isn't it?' But she became quite enthusiastic as she
found forgotten books and dolls. She sobered and held
up an impressively worn teddy bear. 'Its Kewsee.'

'Kewsee?' queried Cara.

'Mum bought him for me when I was about five and I called him Kewsee because people always said that's what Mum would be one day—a Q.C. I wanted to be a Q.C. too, then——' Holly dropped the bear again and closed the drawer on it.

'Hey, look, it's Dad's old bugle,' she called a little later, and lifted the tarnished instrument from its case to blow a horrendous note on it. She discovered several suitcases, checked their contents and rejected them. Mitch came in, grimaced at the smell of mothballs and looked around.

'That's the case——' he began, but Cara caught him back just as Holly reached the suitcase in question.

'Look what we found——' She held out the bugle to him. He took it, turned it over, rubbed a finger over the dents.

'Why don't you play something?' she challenged.

'Don't you think I can?' he grinned, buffing the bugle on his thigh. 'What would you like to hear? It's a bit late in the day for Reveille.'

Holly had the suitcase on the floor and the lid open. She looked over the contents, then her attention was caught and she bent for a closer look.

'Is there a signal for "Advance" or something?' Cara asked softly, and his brow furrowed a little as he lifted the bugle to his mouth. Cara never did ask what he played, but the first notes, squeezed out in reluctance, were followed by several pure ones as Mitch stood there, arms raised, head tilted, and blew a bugle call. Behind him Holly held up a tiny white nightgown, then a bright toy rattle—red and green plastic horses on elastic made to stretch across a baby's pram.

'What do you know,' Mitch laughed, 'I can still do it!' As he blew another long, clear note Holly flexed the elastic and all the tiny horses chattered softly. The white price tag dangled on its white string and she took it between thumb and forefinger and read it. Then she dropped to both knees and delved into the case, seeking and finding all the other small white tags on the small, unused clothes. Holly turned to look up at her father. Mitch lowered his bugle with a reminiscent smile to look down at her.

'These clothes and toys. They're new,' she said huskily and Mitch crouched down and put his arm around her. 'Yes—your mother bought them for the new baby——' he was saying as Cara quietly closed the door on them.

Holly would have to see that no woman, only just pregnant, bought exquisite things for a baby she never intended to have. Would she make the logical extension that if this second child had been eagerly awaited—putting an established, successful career at risk—then she, the first child, must certainly have been wanted? Cara crossed her fingers and hoped this would provide the reassurance Holly needed.

It did.

'Holly has her old teddy bear sitting on her bed,' Mitch told Cara on the phone the next day.

'Kewsee?' asked Cara, relief overflowing. 'Oh, that's fantastic!'

'How did you know, Cara?'

'Holly told me——' People always told her things. Holly, Cleo——

'I wish she'd told me.'

'But you might not have given her convincing reassurance, or so she thought. She preferred to doubt—than to have her doubts confirmed.'

'You stage-managed it beautifully,' he told her. 'Thank you.'

'No need for thanks. I love her too, you know.'

'Holly wants to know how many babies we're going to have.'

She laughed. 'How many babies *are* we going to have?'

'Just a minute—I have a calculator here somewhere——'

Cara played in the Mall with Danny on Friday, her sapphire ring glittering incongruously on the hand that passed around the bowler hat. Mitch's partners, who'd seen her now in crystal blue silk and stiletto heels, laughed at her busking clothes and wild hair.

'Good lord,' one said, 'still performing? Hasn't Mitch put his foot down yet?'

'You'll have to stop all this when you're married to him,' said the other. They were on their way home, attaché cases tucked under their pin-striped sleeves.

'No—no——' she smiled. 'When we're married, Mitch is going to be in charge of the hat.' She waggled the bowler at them and they both guffawed at the tremendous joke.

'Oh, that's good!'

'What a sense of humour!' They went off mightily amused and Cara frowned. It wasn't *that* funny.

More dinners and drinks and a surprise party thrown for them on the glorious patio of someone's glorious riverside home. Cara found herself relaxing more and more. Her new clothes no longer seemed alien. She discovered new ways to match her wits with Mitch's wittiest friends, without treading beyond the bounds of good taste. Mitch was no longer humbled and delighted with her efforts but took it pretty much for granted, and she brushed away her occasional irritation that it was so. She was no longer a child, after all, who needed petting and constant praise for doing what she wanted to do. Making changes wasn't

easy, but Cara discovered new things about herself.
Her free and easy lifestyle had its virtues, but she saw
now that she had sheered away from whole areas of
thinking. Mitch could learn from her, but she could
learn from him too. Her mind sharpened, and she
enjoyed exploring the new territories opening up, and
was happy. Her own friends had a huge party
organised to celebrate the engagement.

'At our place—most of the crowd you met before
will be there. You remember Arty——' she said to
Mitch.

'The fire-eater.'

'—and there are two girls in town that I travelled
with in Greece and Turkey, they're dying to meet
you—and Steve's coming——'

'Steve?'

'You know. He lent us his ropes.'

'Oh, him. The open-air Romeo,' he said drily.

'Jealous?' she grinned, remembering his reaction
when she'd mentioned Cleo. 'Steve's a doll. Just my
type. I don't know why I never fell in love with
him——' Mitch frowned and she laughed. 'But I
didn't. We're just good friends. Anyway, he's coming
because he says he won't believe I'm actually getting
married until he sees the look in my eyes.'

'Hmmph,' grunted Mitch.

'It'll be a fabulous party, better than the last one.
Can you be here early—seven-thirty? I'd like us to
greet everyone together.'

'Hmmm, I don't know——' said Mitch, his brow
deeply furrowed.

'Don't know what?'

'What to wear. I don't think my dinner suit will be
back from the cleaners in time——'

Unlike Pete and Viv's party, which had been a
spontaneous, hurried thing, this party was organised.

Pete brought in a team of his fellow art students and
the flat was transformed with great paper murals
pinned up on the walls—cartoon send-ups of both
Cara and Mitch. Cara with her flute, hair flying
against Parisian street scenes and Greek temples—
Mitch in a dinner suit blowing a bugle, a peacock in
the background. It was touching to see how they'd
remembered the little things she'd let slip about
Mitch. Considering their meagre wages and student
allowances, the food was magnificent. There was a
cake—a double-tiered, super cake decorated by a
friend of a friend of a friend. And there was an
enormous box, gift-wrapped and topped with a gold
bow.

'Everyone chipped in,' Pete told her, 'even Mr
Parini.' Cara laughed a little shakily at that. Mr Parini
the landlord was notoriously tight with his money.
'Oh—and Mario sent the fruit.' It was a massive
basket filled with perfect peaches and mangoes and
one of his best pineapples. No bruised fruit this time.
There was champagne—not the best, but not the worst
either. Cara swallowed a lump in her throat. Her
friends, short of funds as always, had worked together,
used all their resources and given their time to prepare
all this.

'I don't know what to say——' She flung out her
arms as Pete put a cassette in the stereo and started up
the music. 'Wait until Mitch sees it!'

And wait they did. At seven-thirty, when guests
started arriving, Cara greeted them without him.

'He'll be here any minute now——' she said when
they asked, conscious of a tiny surge of irritation that
he was late. Irritation turned to concern when he
hadn't arrived at eight o'clock. She imagined the
Peugeot somewhere overturned—Mitch on a stretcher

being slid into an ambulance. She phoned him twice.
And twice got no answer.

'Probably a flat tyre—I hope his dinner suit doesn't
get dirty,' she quipped, hiding her anxiety.

At eight-fifteen the phone rang. It was Mitch.

'Where *are* you?' she demanded, relief flooding
through her, 'I thought you might have had an
accident——'

'I'm fine,' he assured her.

'How soon can you get here?'

'Cara—I have a slight problem——' He outlined
the slight problem. He was with a client and had
expected to be free in plenty of time for the party, but
things had dragged on.

'It's *Saturday*!' she exclaimed. 'And you could have
phoned!'

'I can't explain, Cara—but phoning would have
been a bit awkward up to now——'

'You could have phoned from your car,' she pointed
out stiffly.

'I didn't come by car. Brewster sent a helicopter to
pick me up.'

'Helicopter! Where are you?'

'I'm on his yacht just off Peel Island. The boat
brought me out at about five and I was hoping to——'
the line faded a bit '—finishing any time now. Sorry,
love. But this is important.'

So was *this*! she wanted to yell. But his voice was
distant and hurried. 'I'll be there just as soon as I can,
okay?' he said, and then there was no voice at all.

Nine o'clock. Cara danced with Pete and drank two
glasses of champagne quickly, one after the other. She
laughed a lot.

'Oh, you know what lawyers are like,' she said when
people asked where Mitch was. 'There's never one
around when you want one.'

Ten o'clock and people stopped asking. The stereo belted out an old Tina Turner number and Cara danced with Steve Roswell. She giggled and talked about old times—'remember when,' she said, remember when they'd first met at a youth hostel in Wales. 'You were a bit of a tearaway, boyo,' she said in a Welsh sing-song. 'And remember when——' She kept her smile and wouldn't meet his eyes, looking again and again at the door. But eventually she looked up at Steve and his kookaburra smile was missing and his bright, laughing eyes were a little sad. She remembered that he'd said he would believe she was getting married when he saw the look in her eyes. 'Sorry, kid,' he said, and drew her close and put his freckled cheek close to hers in consolation.

Eleven o'clock. The cake had been trundled tactfully out of sight. The gift sat unopened. Cara wondered what it was. People stopped making engagement jokes and wedding jokes and avoided Cara's laughing face and her stricken eyes.

It was over before midnight. Cara stood out on Mr Parini's concrete 'lawn' and saw the last car off. Pete and Danny offered her coffee, but she shook her head and stayed out there a long time, leaning by the door, looking up at a million stars. The phone began to ring and she went and stood by it, staring at it. It rang and rang, but she didn't pick it up. The boys came out of their rooms to answer it, baffled when they saw her there. As Danny made to pick up the phone, she held his arm back. 'Leave it,' she said, and looked at the murals and the covered cake and the unopened gift. 'Let it ring.'

She answered it when it rang again in the morning. Mitch would say something, Cara thought—something to excuse his non-arrival. A squall in the Bay—a hole in the yacht's dinghy—the helicopter pilot was sick——

'Cara!' Mitch's voice was warm, a little weary, and she felt weak at the sound. Tell me you couldn't, just couldn't come, she thought, wanting desperately to forgive. You broke a leg—fell on the deck and hit your head and lost your memory.

'I'm sorry, love—I just couldn't get away,' his voice lowered diplomatically. 'Brewster is one of our top clients and when he wants to talk, time is of no consequence.'

Cara straightened. 'I can see that.'

'I did phone you again later, but there was no answer—you wouldn't have heard it, I suppose, over the Rolling Stones,' he chuckled. 'Your parties get noisier as they go along——'

'My parties, Mitch?' She clutched the phone tightly. "*Mine*? This was supposed to be *our* party!'

'I know, and I'm sorry, but this was unavoidable. Brewster——'

'I know. Brewster is *important*.'

There was a small silence as if Mitch was digesting her mood. 'Cara—don't give me flak on this,' he said tiredly, 'I've got enough on my mind. I'm still on the yacht and not finished yet. I'll talk to you as soon as I get back.'

'Should I make an appointment? Would you like to check that out with Superwatch?' she shouted, tears in her eyes.

'Don't be stupid,' he said. 'I love you.'

'And I love you, Mitch. I love you enough to trot along to all those quiet, elegant little drinkies sessions with your partners and dinner with the Judge and visits to your friends—I gave up other things sometimes to go with you, Mitch, I haven't seen much of *my* friends lately because you wanted me to be with you and I wanted it too. Because I love you——'

'Cara——'

'—and I ask you to be with me and my friends *once* and you couldn't make it. Doesn't stand up very well as an equation, does it, Mitch?'

'Equation—what the devil? Look, you have to understand—this is my work——'

'What if I hadn't turned up to meet you for drinks with your partners?' she demanded. 'What if I'd phoned and said, "Sorry, Mitch, can't make it, Danny's written a new song for a band and he needs me to play flute to help him with the arrangement——"'

'Come on, Cara—that's hardly the same thing, is it? This is——'

'I know—important,' she said steadily. 'Like all the social engagements we've had with your friends over the past weeks—*un*like this party that my friends put on for us.'

'That's not——'

'They went to great deal of trouble, Mitch—they haven't money to spare but they spent their time for us—you get that, Mitch? *Time*. You more than anyone should appreciate that.'

'You don't seem to understand,' he sounded tetchy, distracted.

'Oh, I think I'm beginning to get a glimmer,' she shouted, hurt and angry. 'All the compromise is going to be on my side, isn't it? I'm to fit into your world— you're not going to make any effort to fit into mine.'

'For God's sake, Cara, what did you expect? I'm a lawyer with a good practice. Be reasonable!'

'You never had any intention of even trying, did you?' she exclaimed, appalled. 'You just bided your time and knew that because I loved you *I'd* make the changes to make it all work. You—you arrogant

bastard——' The tears rolled down her face now, but
her voice was firm and full of fury. 'I'm to be tamed to
suit your life—I'm to be like one of those poor birds in
your cage, aren't I? Fine feathers and beautiful
surroundings and—and love—but locked away from
the outside——'

'Birds? For God's sake, Cara, you're sounding
hysterical. It's only a party, after all, and there'll be
others. I'll throw one myself as soon as I get back—
invite all your friends to make up for——'

'I won't be locked away, Mitch!' she said, and she
really did feel hysterical then, the tears gushing down
her face. 'I won't!'

She hung up and paced back and forth, dashed
away the tears fiercely, sniffed, avoided the sombre
gaze of the Boobook owl. Danny came out and put his
arm around her and she leaned on him for a moment.

'Damn him,' he muttered. Pete, clad only in pyjama
bottoms, emerged with his chest expander. He pulled
it apart with a mighty heave of his muscled arms.
'Want me to beat him up, Cara?' he asked as the chest
expander sprang back with an angry rattle. Cara gave
a watery laugh.

'That might not be as easy as you think.'

'I'm game,' Pete assured her. 'Teach him a lesson!'

She laughed again. 'Forget it. It's just our first
quarrel——' The boys looked askance at her. 'Well,
the first since we—oh, you know.'

If it were just as simple as that. Deep down she
knew it wasn't. Later she went to the notice board and
looked at the square of paper hanging there. 'Rachel
Elliott,' it said, 'Michael McDade, Sandra Browning.'
Underneath the names was their address in Cairns
and their phone number. Friends of a friend. She
touched the drawing pin that held it in place and the
sapphire ring glittered on her third finger. Her hand

fell away and the square of paper fluttered back against the notice board.

CHAPTER TEN

MITCH phoned again that afternoon.

'I've just got back to the mainland. The chopper is flying me home now. I'll be around to see you at about four.' He sounded bone-weary, and Cara imagined the lines of strain on his face, could almost see him rubbing at his midriff and grimacing. She mellowed with concern, wishing now that she had not lost her temper this morning.

'I love you, Mitch,' she said, but he'd already hung up.

He arrived later than he said. The boys had shown great tact and gone out to give them time alone.

'Hello, Mitch,' she said, emotionally calm now and ready for a quiet, rational discussion on what they both wanted from their marriage. Mitch would be, perhaps, a little regretful. He was a fair man and having had time now to reflect, would be willing to admit that he had concessions to make. He would be showered and rested and recovered from the stress of his all-night session on the yacht and he would . . .

'You really had to make your point, didn't you?' Mitch snarled.

Cara stepped back. He was unshaven; lines of weariness were graven in his forehead and around his mouth, green eyes hard and furious, hands clenched.

'I don't know——'

He stepped inside, slammed the door and Cara winced at the sound. 'Am I supposed to be struck by the symbolism of it all?' he enquired, catching her by the arms.

'Symbolism—Mitch, what are you talking about?'

He shook her. 'Had a change of heart, have you, Cara? Don't want to admit you've done it now? That isn't like you—not straight-from-the-shoulder Ms Matheson who does what she pleases and says what she likes—maybe you've just realised how upset Holly would be——'

He shook her again, gritting his teeth, and Cara's temper rose. With a hand on his chest she pushed.

'Done what? What have I done? And you're hurting——'

'—those birds were her pets. They were her mother's and she loves them and——'

'The birds? Something's happened to the birds?'

Mitch gave a disgusted snort and pushed her away. 'They're all gone—flying around for some of that glorious freedom you value so highly—a day or two of it anyway before they die of starvation or a cat or a dog gets them——' He strode past the wildlife poster, glanced at the Boobook owl, 'Cara the liberator! It must have been a double thrill for you to let them out of their "prison"—return them to the wild and show me exactly how you felt.' He turned on her. 'Well you succeeded—that open door and that empty cage made a very eloquent statement—just as your harem pants and camel bells did once before.'

'It wasn't me, Mitch,' she said unsteadily.

'—marrying me would be entering a prison—isn't that what you were trying to say on the phone this morning? "I won't be locked away," you said, and when I got home the cage was empty.' He gave a mirthless laugh. 'The birds had flown. I'm surprised *you're* still here——'

'Well, I am! And I don't think of marriage as a prison any more,' she told him. 'But marrying you won't work if only one of us makes compromises—my parents failed because neither of them would compromise and my brother tried to learn from their lesson and made *all* the compromises in his two marriages and that didn't work either. I've made some effort to fit into your life, Mitch, but I won't go on trying unless you give me some concessions too.'

'What should I do, Cara?' he said, heavily sarcastic. 'Throw away years of training and a great law practice and become a—a beach bum? Busk on street corners with you?'

She paled, flung her head back. Her hair crackled.

'Would it be so terrible? Tell me, Mitch—you can see me fitting into *your* life—how about seeing yourself fit in with mine? You come and live with *me*—take off Superwatch and stop counting the hours of your life and start living some of them instead. Pack your two pairs of jeans and come hiking through Europe with me the way you always wanted. Holly could come—there are schools—we could travel and work when we wanted and——'

'Don't be ridiculous,' he scoffed.

'Why is it ridiculous? Why?'

'I'm not a kid any more—I can't live that kind of life.'

'And I can't live your life, Mitch. I need you to meet me half-way and you don't seem to be ready or willing to do that, so——'

'So—what now?' he said sarcastically, his jaw clenching and unclenching. 'Will you pack up and move on as usual? Have you come a bit too close this time, Cara—to something approaching a normal life—is it too much for you, the idea of settling down and knowing what to expect next week, next month? Is that what bold, fearless Cara Matheson can't face—predictability?'

His sneer enraged her. Hurt her. 'No, I can't!' she

snapped, thrusting her face up at his. 'I can't face the predictability of seeing you gulp down your breakfast in the few minutes that damned watch allows you between phone calls and seeing your indigestion turn to an ulcer, and I can't face the predictability that you won't be there for me when I need you most because you'll be courting some important client not because you have to but from sheer habit—and I can't face the predictability that I'll *resent* it——'

Mitch gave a rough laugh. 'You're fooling yourself, Cara. You've wanted to run from the first—you dressed up like a slave girl to try to force my hand and give you an excuse, and now I've missed your party, so you'll use that to justify backing off.'

She stared at him. 'No. It isn't me who's being the coward now, Mitch.'

He looked away, face tight with tension. 'This is *stupid*!' he burst out and strode to her, pulling her into his arms. Cara held back, fearing the potency of a physical argument. Already that weak part of her was trying to rationalise, to wave away their differences. It was ironic—once she had wanted excuses to run, as Mitch had said, but now, against all common sense, she was looking for excuses to stay. Mitch pulled her to him, a little roughly, and her arms just somehow went about him and he was kissing her, hurting her mouth with the force of his.

'You can't go——' he muttered, and kissed her again, softer this time, parting her lips persuasively, tongue caressing and exploring. 'Won't let you——' he murmured into her mouth, and his hands swept over her, down to grip her hips possessively, to push up around her ribcage to her breasts. And Cara's eyes closed and she held him and told herself that if they married there was always this—loving him and waking with him every morning; would anything else really matter? Her hand twined in his hair and she kissed him passionately, and the small, cool voice of reason reminding her that love was not always enough grew fainter and fainter——

The phone began to ring. It would stop, she thought, willingly lost in Mitch's arms, but it didn't. They drew apart. Cheeks flushed, lips parted, Cara sidled to the phone without taking her eyes off Mitch. She must be crazy to think of going away. This was just a storm in a teacup . . . she smiled at him, gave a foolish little laugh as he mimed a kiss at her, his eyes heavy-lidded and warm with desire. She felt around for the phone, picked it up and said a rather husky 'Hello', eyes still on Mitch.

'Brewster,' a harsh, male voice announced. 'Put Kirby on the line post haste, will you, that's the girl. It's urgent.'

She blinked, her mind lagging behind in a rich, warm haze.

'Hello?' the voice snapped. 'Kirby is there, isn't he? He said he would be after four——' The rich, warm haze cooled rapidly. Cara came wide awake. Mitch's heavy lids shot up. He looked at his watch and Cara's lips pressed tight together. He had given her number to a client. Her number! So much for a vital, private talk about their future.

'Oh yes, Mr Brewster——' she said, and Mitch came over, hand outstretched to take the phone. She leaned away from him, retaining her hold, and his eyes narrowed. 'Yes, he *was* here, Mr Brewster, but I'm afraid you've missed him, just as I seem to have——' Her gaze never wavered from Mitch's. 'You could try his car telephone. I'm sure you have that number too.' She swallowed hard. 'No, you're not likely to get him at this number again——' She fumbled the receiver back to its rest. Mitch put his hands on his hips, let out a sigh.

'Cara—it was difficult—you have to understand——' His words came to an abrupt halt as she eased the sapphire ring from her finger. Without a tremor she held it out to him.

'Cara——' he implored.

But she dropped the ring in his shirt pocket. Very quietly she said, 'You'd better go, Mitch. You have an important call to take in your car.'

He stood there a moment, his hand clamped over his pocket where the ring made a tiny bump. Then, with an exclamation, he flung away. Almost at the door, he came back to the owl poster, his jaw grinding back and forth. With one goaded, vicious swipe he ripped it from the wall and crushed it in his hands.

'I never could stand that thing staring at me!' he gritted. The door slammed behind him and the crumpled poster crackled and feebly unfolded on the floor. Cara was bent over it, smoothing it out when Pete came in. Her tears flooded over, dripped on the poster. At Pete's horrified stare she began to laugh hysterically. 'Now we know why it's an endangered species,' she giggled while tears poured down her face.

Later she threw the poster away. Then she unpinned the square of paper from the notice board.

It was hot in Cairns. It was nearly always hot in Cairns because it was almost two thousand kilometres closer to the Equator than Brisbane. Around Christmas time the temperatures soared daily into the high thirties, and the beach sands were too hot to walk upon. In shop windows mock reindeer frolicked and artificial snow frosted panes of glass and the boughs of sprightly, false Christmas trees, while cosily clad Santas perspired in shopping malls handing out sweets to near-naked children.

Cara applied to a music academy and a grammar school for a teaching job and in the meantime found work in a tiny café. She moved in with Rachel and Mike and Sandra—friends of a friend. The Mini she had sold to Pete and Viv, and she bought a motor scooter and a bright blue helmet and got a great suntan going to and from work.

On Christmas Day she went to church, then had Christmas dinner on the beach with her flatmates and their friends, and she took a day trip to Green Island one drowsy day before the New Year. In a perfect place beneath coconut palms she sat cross-legged and played her flute while her eyes feasted on the glorious jewel colours of the Coral Sea, the azure sky, the deep purple shadows on white sand. It was magnificent. She, who was always happy, sat in paradise and was miserable.

She had phoned to speak to Holly before she'd left.

'I didn't let your birds out,' she said levelly, and there was a small silence before the girl said, 'Well, I wondered for a while if you'd wanted them to be free, like you said they should be—but I believe you. I think it must have been vandals.' Then she burst out, 'Dad said you're going away—what went *wrong*?'

'Holly, we're very different. Our backgrounds, our friends, the way we like to live——'

Holly brushed aside these major barriers. 'I'll bet he went and accused you of letting the birds out——' she muttered. 'I *told* him not to because he'd be sure to regret it, but he was all uptight about missing your party and because of Mr Brewster, who's a real *meanie* if you know what I mean, and I don't think he was thinking too straight, so Cara, *don't* let that ruin everything——'

'It isn't that, Holly,' said Cara, rather distantly

amused at the idea of the father impulsively ignoring good advice from the daughter—how easily maturity changed hands. 'It would have been nice if he'd thought I wasn't capable of messing with someone else's property, but there are other reasons why it's best that I move on.'

Holly asked Cara to write to her. 'Please, *please*?' she begged, and Cara reluctantly agreed, seeing that this was going to be no simple, clean break. She couldn't just turn her back on Holly, yet it was crazy to be writing letters to her—letters that the girl might read to her father.

'Cara——' Holly had said wistfully, 'I read some-where that sometimes birds that have escaped come back to their cages—do you think that's true?'

It was on the tip of her tongue to ask why they would give up their freedom for a cage again, but she said, 'I don't know, Holly. I suppose you could leave the door open and hope that one or two might find their way back.'

A small silence, more wistful than ever. 'Will *you* come back, Cara?'

She really did try to make a joke of it. 'You make me sound like an escaped bird, too! But don't leave the cage door open for me——' It didn't quite work as humour. Too close to truth to be funny.

A Christmas card came from Holly, wrongly delivered and too late by far for Christmas. From Mitch and Holly, it said, but it was in the girl's handwriting. There was a letter in it too.

'You'll never GUESS!' she wrote, and the excited capitals and underlinings gave the emphasis of Holly's speech. It was like having her there, speaking. 'Snowy came BACK! The very next day after you went away! I left the cage door open and I kept going out to check and there he WAS! He flew out of the cage again when he saw me coming, but he circled around in the trees and came back again, so now we're going to feed him every day and let him stay out and see what happens.'

At this point the letter was dated a few days later in a different pen colour. 'Dear old Snowy just turns up every day, would you believe it? I suppose it's a bit risky and he might not live to be a hundred what with all the cats and stuff roaming around in the outside world, but he seems to like it and comes back for his dinners, so I haven't lost him altogether.' Another new date and the writing changed to red. 'Wait till I TELL you! Cleo turned up here today and dropped a bombshell—and I mean a real megabomb! "I let the birds out," she said, calm as anything, and Dad nearly choked on his coffee. "I'm sorry," she said, but she didn't look THAT sorry. She was acting kind of strange. Good though. Anyone would think someone had let HER out of a cage. (That sounds really weird and I'd cross it out for most people but not for you.) Anyway, when Dad asked her why she did it she said "I think I went a bit crazy. I just had to do it. It was overdue." And she said to tell you that you were right and she had to admit to some hate and do something rotten before she "broke out". (Hope I've got that right.) Well, I suppose she hated poor old Snowy for biting her finger and I suppose the something rotten was letting all Mum's birds out, but I don't know what she meant by breaking out. Her skin looked okay to me. Do you know what she meant?'

Oh yes, Cara knew. Cleo had let it all build up inside her—unaware that Mitch's coming wedding was already on the rocks—and she'd let it all out in a spiteful, childish gesture. The kind of gesture she should have indulged in when she *was* a child. It must have come as a shock to find out that she'd not only freed the birds, but herself.

'Anyway, the thing is, Cleo is going away. She applied for a job in Melbourne and got it. It's for a chain of boutiques and Cleo will have to travel a lot in Europe and America. I feel a bit sorry I was so mean to her. It isn't as if she was ever nasty or anything, but she was always SO nice that she was a bit wimpish and she always treated me like I was a cute little kid of six, but I suppose she wasn't so bad . . .'

The holidays were a bit of a drag, she said. She wished Cara was there . . . remember the rainforest and the abseiling? . . . remember singing in the kitchen? She had invited some friends over and made up a Japanese viewing party in the garden. Her father had gone along too, she said, but he'd stayed out there when they went back to the house, looking up at the stars. She'd started knitting him a sweater. Green to match his eyes. 'I know it's early, but I'm so slow and I want to finish it for winter and when school starts up again I'm going to be flat out catching up on MATHS and ENGLISH—I've decided to do Law when I leave school.' They were going to visit Pa and Nan in Adelaide for two weeks, she said . . .

The letter plagued Cara with vivid pictures. As she served a hamburger to a customer, she would imagine Holly, tongue stuck in the corner of her mouth, working on a slow-growing, gappy sweater—green to match Mitch's eyes. And she would take her turn at the vacuuming at the house and think of Mitch and she wondered if he was still eating lunches with people he disliked and if he thought of her when he stayed outside looking up at the stars, and she wondered if one day he might decide to meet her half-way. And she *did* remember the rainforest and the abseiling. And she *did* remember the singing in the kitchen—and how it felt to be in Mitch's arms and eating croissants in bed, and she tried to kid Rachel and Mike and

Sandra that all that moisture on her face was just perspiration from the exertion of cleaning the floors.

The New Year came in with fireworks and champagne and bagpipes and wore away to late January, and the vivid pictures did not fade. Time heals, people said to her when Guy was killed, and she supposed it had. There would always be a fond place in her heart for Guy—the carefree boy, her first love—but his memory didn't hurt any more. This rawness was created by a living man, and it was more of a loss because of it. January passed humidly into February with summer rain and the tail end fury of cyclone Clive and cyclone Martha. But Clive and Martha were just playing. Along came cyclone Clancy, heading straight for the coast and holding course in spite of all predictions that it would swing away.

They battened down and decided on a bathroom party; the bathroom was the safest room in the house in a cyclone. The worst of the weather hit north of them, blowing away a few roofs, sinking small craft. Power lines went and some telephone lines were out but not theirs. As they drank a little white wine in the bathroom the phone rang and rang, and as the winds and rain had died a little, Cara went to answer it.

'Cara—thank God, you're all right! I've been listening to the radio reports—you were in the path—I thought—Cara?'

It was Mitch. She stood there stupidly, her mouth opening and shutting, her heart thundering at the sound of his voice. 'Mitch,' she said at last in a whisper.

'You *are* all right?' he demanded, his voice rising. 'You sound awful—are you in danger?'

'I'm fine—we're not getting the worst of it—it did veer away at the last minute——'

'Cara, I have to talk to you——' The line faded and

she strained to hear him. Tantalising snippets came to her.

'Been doing a lot of thinking . . . new junior partner . . . time off . . . two pairs of jeans . . .' Could he have said that? '. . . absolutely right . . . a coward and a selfish pig . . .'

'What?' she yelled, dying to hear more about the selfish pig bit. Only gusts of static reached her, and embedded in them, words and phrases that set her heart racketing louder than the storm. 'Travel' and 'backpacks' and 'Greece', she heard, and something about rainforests and smelling flowers. No. Taking time to smell the flowers. He was meeting her half-way.

'I love you,' he shouted over the crackling distance, and she shouted it back to him and followed it with 'I'll get the next coach to Brisbane.' But he was saying something too, and she couldn't make him hear, and then the line went dead altogether and she stood there crying into her glass of white wine.

'Oi, the wind's freshening again. You'd better come back in here just in case,' called Rachel from the bathroom. When she went they all looked with interest at her wet cheeks.

'You crying?' Sandra asked.

'Course she's not,' said Michael. 'That's perspiration, isn't it, honey?'

The telephone lines remained out the next day. Cara picked up a cancelled booking on a coach and it was Friday when she reached Brisbane. She phoned Mitch, wondering if he'd got her telegram. He wasn't in, Valerie told her. Cara's heart sank. Then came the *coup de grâce*.

'Mr Kirby is away on business.'

She gulped. 'Business? When will he be back?'

Monday. Cara put down the receiver and slumped

in the bus terminal phone booth. Away on business. And he must have had her telegram yesterday. Something important must have come up. Something more important than her. You're a devil for punishment, Cara, she thought, and wearily slotted another coin in and dialled.

'Danny,' she said when he answered, 'is there a spare bed there for me tonight?'

He brought her up to date when she arrived at the Red Hill flat. Miss Vernon's hay fever was in abeyance and Mr Parini had fixed the rogue fluorescent.

'The place has no character any more,' he lamented.

'We'll squeeze you in somewhere,' he said when she asked if Viv was using her old room. 'If all else fails—with me,' he added wickedly.

'What would Rhonda say to that?'

He pretended to consider. 'You're right. Take your old room; I withdraw the offer. Rhonda would be upset—I've been telling her my female flatmate was ugly as sin, warts—all that. I'm going to be in big trouble when she sees you.'

'Well, it serves you——' Cara gasped. 'You mean——'

Danny grinned. 'Her sight's coming back. Might never be twenty-twenty, but she can see my baby blues, and she never wanted to be an airline pilot anyway.'

'Danny, that's marvellous! Do you think you and she——?' She lifted a brow.

'Whoa!' Danny held up both hands. 'Let's take this slow and easy, huh? I've only just shaken off my "older woman" phase, you know.'

'Liar. It only lasted two weeks. You young boys are so flighty.'

'Love you,' he said softly, 'like a brother. Honest.'

Cara kissed him on the cheek, like a sister. Later, as she unzipped her bag to take out a few things, Danny leaned in the doorway of her old room.

'Want to play with me tonight in the Mall—just like old times?'

Her heart gave an odd, painful jump. Old times. It wasn't so very long ago that she'd played there. Five months, was it? Nearly five months since she'd first passed Mitch by on the escalator—seen·him come out on to the Southdown Building steps and look at that damned watch. 'No.'

'Afraid you'll run into Mitch?'

'That's the last thing I'm afraid of,' she said drily, 'I thought we had a reconciliation going—that's why I'm here. I sent him a telegram to say I was coming but—he's gone away on business.'

Danny frowned. 'I wouldn't have thought he was a man to make the same mistake twice.'

'Neither would I.'

'He's been asking about you. I talked Pete out of beating him up,' he smiled. 'Mitch looked like a man with change on his mind.'

'I thought that too,' she sighed. Silence fell for a while.

'So will you play with me? I've got Samantha back, but I'm hanging on to my busker's licence to pay for some modifications.'

'How do you know I've brought my flute?'

'You always bring your flute.' He strolled over and looked into the bag. 'And the hat too, I'll bet.'

Cara pulled the bowler out from the bottom of the bag and knuckled out the dents in it.

'Why do you always carry it?' he asked.

She smiled. It had been Guy's. She never found out where he'd got it, but it had been battered when first she saw it. 'Oh, for sentimental reasons, I suppose—

it's connected with so many things—a way of life——'
  'Symbolic?'
  'Maybe.' Of carefree days and nights and laughter
and fun and living for each day with no for evers—the
laughter and the fun echoed down the years a little
hollowly, like the sounds of her flute and Guy's violin
heard in a Metro tunnel a long, long time ago. 'Sure,'
she said. 'I'll play. I've nothing else to do.'
  The Mall was lit already, for the dusk came earlier
now in the last segment of summer. School had started
again and clusters of students devoured McDonald's
french fries and Hungry Jack's burgers. There were
girls in long dresses and short dresses and boys
wearing jackets that looked as if they belonged to their
fathers—and some wearing jackets that looked as if
they belonged to their mothers. There were meandering families and locked-together lovers. The electronic
billboard erased a message in clacking monotone and
began weaving a new one. Down on Arty's corner a
column of flame flared.
  'Danny Brand, ladies and gentlemen—one day
you'll have to pay big bucks to hear him—right now
he's here playing beautiful music for you for a mere
coin—thank you, madam—thank you, sir——'
  They let the crowd go and took a break. A great
depression took hold of Cara. It was a tremendous
effort to smile and play music. Up there on the twelfth
floor was Mitch's empty office. Perhaps all those
isolated words and phrases she'd heard on the phone
were the product of a wishful imagination. Must have
been. He was away on business. She looked over from
habit when the bronze glass doors opened. But it was
Mitch's partner, Richard Greenway, who emerged.
He looked startled to see her—came hurrying down
the steps.

'What are you doing here, Cara?' he wanted to know.

Missing Mitch. Again. 'Just—visiting friends,' she said drily.

'But Mitch flew up to Cairns yesterday after noon——'

She stared at him. 'Valerie said he'd gone away on business.'

'Yes—well—it sounds better, doesn't it?'

Cara caught his arm. 'You mean he flew up to Cairns to see *me*? I'm the business?' Richard nodded. Cara threw an arm around his neck and planted a kiss on his cheek.

'Oh, thanks, Rich——' she said, to his surprise, and promptly forgot about him. 'Danny, I have to get to a phone—ring Rachel and see if Mitch went there—leave a message at his house—*something*. Can I have some of these?'

Scooping up a handful of coins from his guitar case, she skittered off, her flute under one arm, the bowler hat pressed to her chest. All the phones in the Mall were in use. Feverishly she waited, but the callers were a long way from fond farewells. Frustrated she looked around for a red phone, took the steps up into the Wintergarden complex, eyes darting around frantically. Maybe on the next level . . . she stepped on to the escalator and stood there hemmed in, staring at the heels and shopping bags of the woman in front of her, thinking of Mitch flying to Cairns to see her—and her rushing down here to see him. And *missing* each other! 'Oooh,' she groaned in the back of her throat. The woman in front made a half turn of her head, shuffled a little uneasily on the moving stairs. Cara looked beyond her, anxious to reach the next level. All the passengers on the downward escalator were busy avoiding eye-contact. Eyes front, all of them.

Except for one man. His gaze wandered, just as Cara's did. They saw each other in the same instant.

'Mitch!' she breathed, and the woman in front gathered her parcels protectively close. Cara saw her name on his lips and suddenly nothing mattered but reaching him. She laughed a little and tears sprang to her eyes. It was fine, it was okay—Mitch was coming to her, she was going to him. She leaned over the escalator side, reached out a hand to him. 'Mitch, I came by bus—and thought you'd gone away on business——'

He caught at her hand. 'I flew up to Cairns and thought you'd moved on again—then I couldn't get another flight out——' The contact was breaking as the escalators took them their separate ways. Both strained to hold on, but their hands dragged apart and they turned to watch the other carried away. Cara felt an illogical sense of panic. She was *missing* Mitch again!

'Did you mean it about Greece and hiking and taking time off?' she called after him.

'Thought you might fancy it as a honeymoon,' he yelled back. Nobody was eyes-front any more. The passengers' heads turned to follow the exchange between the girl on her way up and the man on his way down. 'Wait for me——' Cara craned to peer past the fascinated faces of the passengers behind her. 'I'll come down to you.'

Mitch was saying something too, but she didn't hear. When she rushed around to take the other escalator down again, she realised it must have been—'Wait for me, I'll come up to you.' For there he was riding up again as she travelled down. She began to laugh. So did he. They were carried towards each other again and again they leaned over, reached out to touch.

'I'm sorry I accused you of letting the birds escape——' he said as their fingers brushed.

'I'm sorry I said you were a coward,' she replied, swivelling as he slid upwards, past her.

'Will you show me the way to Andreas' village in Greece?' he called down.

'I might get lost again.'

He cupped his hand around his mouth. 'I'm counting on it——' And the new passengers turned to catch this odd conversation while the last load of passengers lingered on the upper and lower levels to see what the outcome might be. Cara vaguely noticed all the faces, the whispers, the smiles. She felt panicky again—as if she and Mitch might go on passing each other by, having the joy of being carried together, then a mere tantalising touch before they were taken in opposite directions. Oh God, she thought, tears springing anew—her parents had spent all their lives on an escalator ride—going in opposite directions. There was a ripple of laughter from the upstairs gallery—a concerted 'Oooh!' such as a circus audience might make, then there was a shuffle of feet on the down escalator—a parting of people like tall wheat cut through by a breeze. Only it wasn't a breeze coming through. It was Mitch, and suddenly he was there beside her on the same step, going in the same direction.

'Mitch—you climbed over! That's dangerous!' she squeaked as his arm went around her.

'Brushing up my abseiling skills,' he said.

'It's illegal, too,' she murmured as his other arm went around her.

'Know where I can find a good lawyer?' he asked as her arms wound around his neck and the bowler hat was crushed between them.

'I know one,' she whispered, and kissed him. The

stairway carried them down and their feet found solid
ground, but their kiss went on and the other
passengers flowed off around them, grinning.

Mitch raised his head, smiled down at her. 'I know
we needed to meet half-way—but I was beginning to
think it might keep us apart for ever. I went to you—
you came to me—you went up—I went down—for a
while there I thought I was in some kind of hell where
we both wanted each other so much that we'd just
keep on——'

'Missing?' She touched his face tenderly. 'We won't
do that, will we, Mitch? We won't let it become an
escalator ride?'

'Only if we're going the same way.'

'Which way?' she asked softly.

'Our way.'

'Can we do it?'

'Some of your way, some of mine——' he paused,
smoothed back her hair. 'When I first met you, I
began to see that I'd only been half living—it was like
having a new pair of eyes. I'd got so caught up in work
that I'd never really made time to stop and question
where I was going and why. It's a pretty painful
process to shake at the foundations of your life, and I
suppose knowing you made me realise I had to do it.
But then suddenly I *had* you—you loved me and you
began to fit into my life, and because you were there
you made it all seem more bearable, so I—just didn't
face up to facts after all. That's what I've been doing
all this time—sorting myself out.' He looked rueful.
'You were right—I was being the coward in the end.
And I was also——'

'A selfish pig?'

Mitch looked enquiringly at her. 'Did I say that?'

'You did.'

'Rash of me.'

'You seem to be getting more rash all the time—haring off to Cairns on a "business trip"—leaping from escalator to escalator——' she grinned, eyed his travel-crumpled shirt open at the neck, his jaw just beginning to show the need for a shave, '—even leaving off your tie.'

'See what you've done to me!' he laughed.

'Mmmm. I love it.'

They became aware at last of the crowds, impatient now, pushing past them, and strolled away, arms around each other, Cara with her flute and hat stuck under one arm.

'Why were you up there, anyway?' she asked suddenly. 'On the escalator coming down.'

'Mmmmm? Oh, I parked my car up in the Wintergarden car park. I phoned your old flat from the airport but there was no answer so I drove here, figuring I'd speak to Danny in the Mall——'

Danny had a crowd gathered again. 'Danny Brand's the name, ladies and gentlemen,' he was saying as a few coins plonked into his guitar case. 'Here every Friday night——' He looked over at Cara and Mitch and winked. '—playing simply *magnificent* music for you—and now here's a request number. An oldie but a goldie——' He pushed his cowboy hat back on his forehead and played a jazz intro. 'She gets too hungry for dinner at eight——' he sang, and Mitch groaned.

'I'll never live it down, will I?'

'Never.'

'I love you,' he said, so softly that it was just a movement of his lips.

'She never bothers with people she hates——'

'I love you, Mitch.' She reached up to kiss him. 'I can see Holly coming——' she said dreamily, looking over his shoulder. A slender, uniformed figure ambled down the Mall with Kay Leslie close behind.

'That's why the lady is a tramp——'

'Good—we can go home,' Mitch said, and he kissed her again. As his mouth touched hers, Cara saw Holly come to a stop, then throw something up in the air.

'*Wow*!' she shouted. The sound rang up and down the Mall. Arms around each other, they began to walk towards the running girl.

Cara left the bowler hat on the step. There were two coins in it. And Superwatch. Beeping.

Happy Mother's Day.

This Mother's Day, instead of the usual breakfast in bed, why not ask your family to treat you to the Mills & Boon Mother's Day pack. Four captivating romances to enthral you.

THE EMERALD SEA by Emily Spenser

A marine biologist finds herself out of her depth on an Italian film set — and with the director.

THE MARRIAGE BED by Catherine George

A holiday in the Algarve becomes a nightmare when the heroine is kidnapped in revenge for an injustice she knows nothing about.

AN IDEAL MATCH by Sandra Field

Despite two broken engagements, a young woman still believes in marriage — she comes to love a widower left with three children but finds he had lost his faith in love.

ROUGH DIAMOND by Kate Walker

Can a successful businesswoman and a garage mechanic really bridge the gap between two such different backgrounds?

FOUR UNIQUE LOVE STORIES IN A SPECIAL MOTHER'S DAY PACK AVAILABLE FROM FEBRUARY 1987.

PRICE £4.80.

AND THEN HE KISSED HER...

This is the title of our new venture — an audio tape designed to help you become a successful Mills & Boon author!

In the past, those of you who asked us for advice on how to write for Mills & Boon have been supplied with brief printed guidelines. Our new tape expands on these and, by carefully chosen examples, shows you how to make your story come alive. And we think you'll enjoy listening to it.

You can still get the printed guidelines by writing to our Editorial Department. But, if you would like to have the tape, please send a cheque or postal order for £2.95 (which includes VAT and postage) to:

- -

AND THEN HE KISSED HER...

To: Mills & Boon Reader Service, FREEPOST, P.O. Box 236, Croydon, Surrey CR9 9EL.

Please send me _____ copies of the audio tape. I enclose a cheque/postal order*, crossed and made payable to Mills & Boon Reader Service, for the sum of £_____.

*Please delete whichever is not applicable.

Signature _____

Name (BLOCK LETTERS) _____

Address _____

_____ Post Code _____

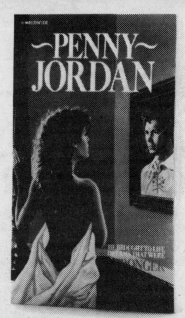

Bewitched in her dreams she awoke to discover the face of reality

The same dark hair, the same mocking eyes.
The Regency rake in the portrait, the seducer of Jenna's dreams had a living double.

But James Allingham was no dream, he was a direct descendant of the black sheep of the Deveril family.

They would fight for the possession of the ancestral home. They would fight against desire to be together.

Unravel the mysteries in
STRONGER THAN YEARNING,
a new longer romance from
Penny Jordan.

AVAILABLE FROM FEBRUARY 1987. PRICE £2.95. **W⊕RLDWIDE**

ACCEPT 4
MILLS & BOON
ROMANCES
ABSOLUTELY FREE

...after all, what better way to continue your enjoyment of the finest stories from the world's foremost romantic authors? This is a very special introductory offer designed for regular readers. Once you've read your four **free** books you can take out a subscription (although there's no obligation at all). Subscribers enjoy many special benefits and all these are described overleaf. ►►►

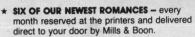

As a regular subscriber you'll enjoy

★ **SIX OF OUR NEWEST ROMANCES** – every month reserved at the printers and delivered direct to your door by Mills & Boon.

★ **NO COMMITMENT** – you are under no obligation and may cancel your subscription at any time.

★ **FREE POSTAGE AND PACKING** – unlike many other book clubs we pay all the extras.

★ **FREE REGULAR NEWSLETTER** – packed with exciting competitions, horoscopes, recipes and handicrafts... plus information on top Mills & Boon authors.

★ **SPECIAL OFFERS** – specially selected books and offers, exclusively for Mills & Boon subscribers.

★ **HELPFUL, FRIENDLY SERVICE** – from the ladies at Mills & Boon. You can call us any time on 01- 684 2141.

With personal service like this, and wonderful stories like the one you've just read, is it really any wonder that Mills & Boon is the most popular publisher of romantic fiction in the world?

*This attractive white canvas tote bag, emblazoned with the Mills & Boon rose, is yours absolutely **FREE**!*

Just fill in the coupon today and post to:
MILLS & BOON READER SERVICE, FREEPOST,
PO BOX 236, CROYDON, SURREY CR9 9EL.

FREE BOOKS CERTIFICATE

To: Mills & Boon Reader Service, FREEPOST,
PO Box 236, Croydon, Surrey. CR9 9EL
Please note readers in Southern Africa write to:
Independant Book Services P.T.Y., Postbag X3010, Randburg 2125, S. Africa

Please send me, free and without obligation, four specially selected Mills & Boon Romances together with my free canvas Tote Bag – and reserve a Reader Service Subscription for me. If I decide to subscribe I shall receive six new Romances each month for £7.20 post and packing free. If I decide not to subscribe, I shall write to you within 10 days. The free books and tote bag are mine to keep in any case. I understand that I may cancel or suspend my subscription at any time simply by writing to you. I am over 18 years of age.

Please write in BLOCK CAPITALS

Name _____

Address _____

_____ Postcode _____

Signature _____
Please don't forget to include your postcode.

SEND NO MONEY NOW – TAKE NO RISKS

The right is reserved to refuse application and change the terms of this offer.
Offer expires September 30th 1987 and is limited to one per household. Harlequin is an imprint
of Mills & Boon Ltd. You may be mailed with other offers as a result of this application.
Offer applies in UK and Eire only. Overseas send for details.

EP32R